Pretty as a Peach
A Sex and Sweet Tea Novel

SAWYER BENNETT WRITING AS
Juliette Poe

ISBN: 978-1-940883-77-9

Find Juliette on the web!
Website: juliettepoe.com
Twitter: twitter.com/juliette_poe
Facebook: facebook.com/AuthorJuliettePoe

Table of Contents

CHAPTER 1 1

CHAPTER 2 8

CHAPTER 3 16

CHAPTER 4 24

CHAPTER 5 30

CHAPTER 6 37

CHAPTER 7 46

CHAPTER 8 54

CHAPTER 9 62

CHAPTER 10 70

CHAPTER 11 78

CHAPTER 12 84

CHAPTER 13 93

CHAPTER 14 102

CHAPTER 15 112

CHAPTER 16 121

CHAPTER 17 130

CHAPTER 18 136

CHAPTER 19 143

CHAPTER 20 152

CHAPTER 21 160

CHAPTER 22 168

CHAPTER 23 175

CHAPTER 24 182

CHAPTER 25... 189

CHAPTER 26... 196

CHAPTER 27... 204

CHAPTER 28... 211

CHAPTER 29... 217

About the Author 227

CHAPTER 1

Darby

T HE MILES PASS by slowly, made even more painful by the fact Linnie will not talk to me. The back of her head rests against the car seat, and she stares blankly out of the windshield. She's been in that position ever since we left our home in Illinois over four hours ago. As we were pulling out of our driveway, I told her not to look back.

Apparently, she took me at my word.

"Want to stop and get a late breakfast when we hit Indianapolis?" I ask my seven-year-old daughter pleasantly, hoping to transfer some positive attitude to her.

She doesn't respond.

"I know you have to be hungry."

Crickets.

"Are you just going to never talk to me again? I mean, when you need something, how are you going to convey it? Are you going to point at food and assume I'll know you're hungry? Or maybe you'll start communicating with grunts?"

When I take my eyes off the road briefly to give her a playful smirk, I get nothing in return.

With a heavy sigh, I turn up the radio slightly, trying to listen to the words of some meaningless song that has no chance in hell of taking my mind off my daughter's sadness.

She's heartbroken to be leaving the only home she's ever known. Once I made my decision to relocate to North

Carolina, she did nothing but beg and plead me with me not to. I had to hear about how much she would miss her friends, her school, her horse, and her father. The friends, horse, and school I totally understood.

Her dad? I can't quite figure that one out. Deep down, I think she's laying it on extra thick about her father to hurt me a bit for making her leave. Linnie and her dad are not overly close, so she has an ulterior motive for sure.

In the two months I have been separated from Mitch, I can count on one hand the number of nights she has spent with him. He's always too busy with his career and travel. This was no different than how things were throughout the course of our nine-year marriage. The reality is Mitch was never a very "present" father in either the literal or figurative sense. Sure, he provided us with a beautiful house and bought Linnie a horse when she was five. He's taken us on extravagant vacations, and pretty much bought our daughter anything she ever wanted. But past that, he just doesn't know how to be connected in the most important ways with our child. It's why it's baffling to me how she's suddenly using him as a "need" for us to stay. She makes me feel like I'm traumatizing her by moving away from him, but in truth, she's not losing out on a lot of interaction with him.

"I have to go to the bathroom," Linnie says and because it's been hours since I heard her voice, I jump slightly from the surprise of it.

I turn to her with such a bright, hopeful smile on my face that she even bothered to ask me for something. She rolls her head on the seat toward me, glaring from behind her glasses. My smile falters.

Turning back to the road, I spy an exit with several gas stations coming up. "I'll pull off up here. We can also grab something to eat if you want."

She doesn't reply.

I take my foot off the gas and naturally slow as I approach the exit. I'm pulling a small U-Haul trailer behind my old BMW Mitch bought me seven years ago, and I've been nervous as hell. I've been driving a lot slower than I normally would, but I'm terrified the darn thing is going to rip loose from the back of my car or something.

After I pull into the gas station, deciding to go ahead and top off my tank, I steel myself to have some type of heart-to-heart with Linnie because I'll never survive the next eleven hours on the road with her like this.

Linnie takes off her seatbelt and starts to open the door. I put my hand on her arm and say, "Wait just a minute."

My daughter flops back into the seat with a pained sigh and stares out of the windshield. Her lips are pressed flat together, and she crosses her arms over her chest.

The message is clear. We are still in battle mode.

I take a calming breath to keep my anger in check. This has been extremely difficult for her. I keep reminding myself that outside of the last few weeks, Linnie and I have a beautifully strong and loving relationship. I take my fingertips and rub them across her brow, bringing my hand down to the back of her neck where I squeeze it gently. "Honey... I know how hard this is on you, and I wish I could do something—"

Linnie's head snaps my way, her eyes all round and hopeful from behind her thick glasses that showcase her baby blues that match my own. She's been wearing them for four years now, and I think they make her look adorable. She hates them with an undying passion and can't wait until the day she's old enough to have contacts.

"Let's just go back," she says earnestly. "Please, Mom, we

can make this work if we go back. I know Daddy would take us back."

I'm shaking my head before she can even get out the last words because we've had this discussion before.

Numerous times.

"No, baby. We can't make it work."

"But Daddy will take us back," she pleads.

"I know, honey," I tell her sadly. "But *I* can't go back."

Linnie takes an index finger and pushes her glasses up her nose. "You're not even trying. You didn't even try to make it work."

I don't respond to her because she's only seven, and she has no clue how long I tried to make it work. She'll never understand the pieces of myself I abandoned in the early years of our marriage to keep Mitch happy. She'll never understand the sacrifices I made to give her a good life.

I harden my voice slightly, so she understands we can't keep going around and around about this. "Linnie... listen to me. I know this seems impossibly difficult right now, but it will get better. We'll settle into our new place, and you'll meet new friends."

She turns around with a huff of frustration and glares out the passenger window, effectively telling me she doesn't want to listen to a damn thing I have to say.

My lungs expand with an automatic sigh followed by a tiny flash of anger-laced frustration that she won't even give me an inch. I stifle that sigh, though, and tell her, "I'm done talking about going back. I understand your position, and I hope that you understand mine. But this is happening whether you like it or not."

Her head whips back to me, causing her glasses to slide down her nose again. She automatically pushes them up, which I bet she must do a hundred times a day. She stares hatefully and the enmity in her eyes takes me aback. Her voice is low and harsh. "Then take me back and let me live with Dad. I don't want to live with you."

The other thing Linnie will never understand at age seven is the power that words have over people. Hopefully, it will be a very long time before she ever feels the intense ache in the center of her chest—like I have right this minute—when someone she loves tells her something hurtful.

What I would really like to tell her is the truth. I would like to take her face in my hands, get up close to her, and tell her the God-awful truth that her father would not want her to live with him. That he does not have the time nor the inclination to raise a child, and those were his exact words when I tried to work out custody arrangements with him. I would love to make her understand he had not one single qualm about Linnie moving. Sure, he was completely irate and affronted *I* would leave him, but Linnie just didn't matter. A child to Mitch is nothing more than arm candy. It's a way for him to show his cronies he has a beautiful family and it's all his doing.

No, I will never let Linnie know what a bastard her father is. So I only say, "Well, I love you more than the air I breathe, and I need you with me. And your father agreed to it. So that's just the way it's going to be."

I get another glare from her, and then she's pushing her way out the passenger door. She slams it behind her and leans against the car, her arms once again crossed over her chest to remain in her battle posture.

I have a moment of great weakness, and I consider the possibility of returning to Mitch. To give up all of my hopes and dreams so my daughter can have her friends and her horse. I think about how it wouldn't be so bad to endure his verbal abuse, crazy possessiveness, and constant shaming. Certainly, I could look past the mistress I recently found out about.

My eyes cut to the rearview mirror and the ones staring back at me look utterly defeated.

It would be so easy to give in.

My phone rings, startling me, and I grab it from the center console. I see from the screen it's my older sister Kelly, and I don't hesitate to answer. "Hey."

"Just checking in to see where you are," she says, and I immediately feel my resolve bolstering just from her voice. Kelly has been an immense source of strength to me since I decided to leave Mitch.

"I'm just outside of Indianapolis," I tell her as I pull the key out of the ignition. "We're just now stopping for gas and a bathroom break."

"How is Linnie?" she asks hesitantly. Kelly is well aware her niece has been fighting me every step of the way with this move.

I give a forlorn sigh into the phone that probably tells Kelly all she needs to know. "She fluctuates between silence and open hostility. I'm not sure how to deal with either."

"You know how to deal with both because you are the best mom in the world," my sister tells me, and the surety in her voice bucks me up even further. "Just give her time, Darby. That's all she needs."

Yes. That's all she needs, and it's all I need as well. I just need time and distance. Hopefully my life will get back on track, and both of us will be the better for it.

When my former brother-in-law—Kelly's ex-husband— offered me the chance of a lifetime to move to North Carolina and become his operations manager for a farm he had just purchased, there was no way I could say no. It was my chance to break away from Mitch.

Even though Kelly and Jake have been divorced for more than a year, they remained the closest of friends. It's quite remarkable how well they get along since the divorce, and that's evidenced by the fact Kelly is his right-hand man in the multimillion-dollar tech company he owns.

Jake bought the farm in Whynot, North Carolina to help me out of a bad situation. Oh, he will tell anyone who will listen that it's purely for the tax break, but he never even thought about such a thing until I spilled my guts to Kelly about how badly I needed out of my marriage.

About how badly Mitch was starting to scare me.

While I never intended for Kelly to run to Jake with my problems, in hindsight I can't regret it. Jake jumped into action, and now I'm on my way to a new and better life for both me and Linnie.

I know one day she will appreciate it.

CHAPTER 2

Colt

AFTER I FINISH stocking the last case of Miller Lite, I take all the empty boxes out to the recycle bin in the back alley. Once back inside, I give the old wooden floors a good wet mop and I'm ready to open the doors for business.

I'm pulling a double shift at Chesty's today since the regular day bartender, Sam Pete, has a "summer cold". That translates into a hangover because for one, it's fall, not summer, and last night was his girlfriend's twenty-first birthday. Pap called me this morning to tell me Sam Pete was in a bad way, and he wanted to know if I could cover. I don't mind because I remember what it was like to be that age. Plus, I take every opportunity I can to earn money.

It's true I live rent-free in a cabin my brother built on Mainer Farm. But for the last two years, I have foregone the salary that would ordinarily be paid to me as the farm foreman because, sadly, Mainer Farms is struggling.

Mama and Dad have no clue I haven't been taking my salary because in addition to overseeing the regular operations, I also handle the books, so I've kept that very much a secret. They don't need the stress of that knowledge. Besides, my parents have busted their butts working that farm for so many years they deserve to kick back and relax a bit.

The farm is going to be mine one day, so I don't mind investing the sweat equity into it. I love my heritage as an eighth-generation farmer in my hometown of Whynot. My siblings have all chosen different career paths, and I'm thankful for that. That leaves Mainer Farms strictly under my control, which is just how I like it. I have grand plans to pull us up by the bootstraps, and it would be a total pain in the ass if I had to run everything by my brother and sisters before I could act.

As I step behind the bar, I note the top didn't get scrubbed down last night when Felicia closed. She's a new bartender Pap recently hired, but she's lazy as all get out. I fill up the sink with soapy water, and then proceed to wipe down the sticky beer that was spilled by last night's drunks.

The front door to the bar opens, and Pap ambles in. He's eighty-two and had surgery almost four weeks ago to remove part of his colon because he has cancer. Looking at him now, though, he looks as fit and spry as he ever did. As a former Marine drill instructor, he carries himself with his shoulders thrown back and his chin lifted in the air like he's almost daring someone to take him on. I would not want to get into a scuffle with the old coot.

"Give me a beer," Pap growls as he takes his seat at the end of the twelve-foot bar.

I grin as I pull a fresh mug out of the freezer and hold it under the tap. "It's only eleven o'clock in the morning."

"So?" he challenges me belligerently. "What's your point?"

I shrug and slide the beer toward him. "Just saying… Most folks are still drinking their coffee at this time of day."

Pap picks up his beer. He holds it up to me in a mock toast and says with an exaggerated, fake southern drawl, "Well, I ain't most folk."

"Look at you," I praise him with a laugh. "Using good old southern words like 'ain't'. Proud of you."

He snorts and takes a slug from his beer. He's been in Whynot for over twenty years, but still sounds like a Pittsburgher.

Snickering, I turn to the cash register. Pulling out my wallet, I tell him over my shoulder, "This one's on me."

After I pay for his beer—because no one drinks free here—I close the register and face him again.

I give him a critically closer look and note he looks damn good. His face is full of color, and he looks to be brimming with the same piss and vinegar that makes up most of his personality.

"What are you looking at?" he grumbles.

I shrug. "Just making sure you're not gonna keel over during my watch."

Pap snorts. "I'm going to outlive all you kids."

I nod. That's probably the God's honest truth. The swinging glass door opens again, and Pap and I turn to see my sister, Laken, walking in.

"Want a beer?" I ask.

She shakes her head as she takes the adjacent seat next to Pap. "Got any coffee made?"

I don't respond, but move to the forty-cup pot I put on about ten minutes ago. Even though this is a bar, we still get plenty of people who come in and just want to drink coffee. I expect it's because the southern teetotalers don't want alcohol, but clearly enjoy the company inside of Chesty's. Pap is a major source of entertainment and good, honest conversation in our small town.

I put Laken's coffee in front of her after I doctor it up just the way she likes it with plenty of cream and sugar.

"What you are doing today?" Pap asks her. I lean against the counter that runs behind me, and then cross my arms over my chest as well as one leg over the other at the ankle.

"Jake's flying in this morning from Chicago," she tells us, and I can't help but notice the sparkle in her eyes when she mentions his name. "He's going to meet me here, and then we're going to go have lunch at Central Café before heading out to the farm. Got to get a few things in order because Darby and Linnie are going to be arriving today."

At the mention of the name Darby, my skin tightens and my jaw locks. I've never met Jake's former sister-in-law, who is going to be running Farrington Farms for him, and I'm not sure I ever want to meet her. I'm still nursing a lot of sore feelings over the fact she applied for the same expansion grant that I did from the North Carolina Department of Agriculture.

My bootstrap idea to save Mainer Farms has been in the works a long time. I've been developing a long-term plan to open a winery as part of Mainer Farms. The first step is to plant the grapes. It will take a few years for them to mature and be able to harvest. That expansion grant is crucial to my plans, and my plans are crucial to keep Mainer Farms operating.

I know this Darby-woman has every right to apply for that grant, but it still sticks in my craw that she did it because she doesn't really need it.

Not the way I do.

Jake bought Farrington Farms for a tax write-off. He expects to lose money. My understanding from Laken, who irritatingly defends Jake and Darby, is she had to apply for the grant in order to meet the requirements of her thesis. Darby is apparently a smarty-pants who is trying to finish her PhD in agronomy.

So essentially, she's doing it to write a paper while I'm

doing it to save my family's farm.

"Once that girl gets settled in, you bring her by here for beer," Pap instructs Laken.

Laken beams a sweet smile at her grandpa. "I will. I'll also invite her to one of our Sunday dinners. I imagine she's going to be overwhelmed and lonely, so I want to show her some good Mainer hospitality."

Technically, our family name is Mancinkus. It's Pap and my dad's surname. But truth is, when we talk about hospitality, we talk about my mama's side of the family. We're southern through and through and having people over for Sunday dinner is just a way of life for us.

Laken shoots me a pointed look, but I ignore it.

"How old is her daughter?" Pap asks. I listen with only half an ear because I really couldn't care less.

"She's seven years old," Laken replies. "Darby is going to enroll her over at Height Elementary on Monday."

For someone who doesn't even care, I can't help myself from commenting, "That means she'll get Mrs. Nicholson."

Laken nods while wrinkling up her nose in distaste. All of us Mancinkus kids had Mrs. Nicholson for the second grade, and not one of us liked her. She wore way too much rose perfume and her voice was overly squeaky when she yelled.

And Mrs. Nicholson yelled a lot. Why somebody with her bad temperament chose to teach children who are often unruly at that age is beyond me.

Laken turns her head and gives me a sweet, imploring look. "Hey, Colt... Would you be willing to come over tomorrow and help us get Darby's stuff unloaded? She's going to be pulling in late tonight, so I figured we would unpack in the morning."

I'm shaking my head out of pure stubbornness and unwillingness to help the woman who is going to make my life a little more difficult. It's a crappy thing to do and totally not indicative of the southern hospitality to which I have been raised in, but I tell her, "Sorry. Got plans already."

Laken arches an eyebrow at me. "Oh, really? Like what?"

"Nunya," I tell her.

Her eyebrows furrow in confusion, and Pap snickers under his breath. "Nunya?"

"Yeah, none ya business," I tell her as I push off from the counter and walk over to the refrigerator that sits between the beer cooler and a small toaster oven we use to cook frozen pizzas.

"You don't have plans," she taunts at my back. I open the fridge and pull out a bottle of water. "You're just sore at Darby for no reason at all."

"I've got reason," I mutter as I twist off the cap and take a long swallow.

"What's his reason?" Pap asks curiously. With him facing cancer and surgery, he's not been in the gossip loop lately.

"Darby applied for the same grant Colt wants," Laken explains. "And he's acting like a third grader over it."

"Am not," I mutter.

"Well, you were an ass to Jake," she points out. And yeah… I was a little hot headed when I found out about it and confronted the man who I really knew nothing about. Only that he was a hotshot Yankee businessman come to town who had no business becoming a farmer.

I mean… running a farm at a loss? It's almost a slap in the face to us farmers who work eighty hours a week to eke out a living.

But I'll have to admit I've since come to like Jake. I'll grudgingly admit he's got a good heart and most importantly, he makes my sister happy.

Doesn't mean I have to like Darby, though. Or help her. As far as I'm concerned, she's the competition and that makes her my enemy.

So no… I won't be helping.

Besides, I really do have important plans that are none of Laken's business. I'm heading over to Duplin County to meet with a vintner there who runs a successful winery.

Yes, we make wine in the South. I know Californians look down their nose at us, but our muscadine grapes—scuppernong being the main variety I intend to grow—make a very distinctive and purely unique tasting wine. This Duplin vintner makes quite a good living at it, and I intend to tour his vineyard today. He was kind enough to let me pick his brain some.

"Colt… seriously," Laken continues to push at me. "Please come help unload Darby tomorrow. I'll make dinner and—"

"I really can't," I say as I turn back to her, my voice softening so she understands this isn't a childish reaction to the grant situation. "I really do have plans, and I can't discuss them with you until I know if it's something that's plausible."

Plausibility rests solely with me getting that grant.

At this, Laken sits up straighter and Pap leans toward me. They know I'm working my fingers to the bone to make Mainer Farms successful again, and they have figured out that whatever I'm doing tomorrow is for *ye olde homestead.*

"When will you share with us?" she asks curiously. "You know we can help out."

Yes, I know any of my siblings would do whatever was necessary to keep the farm from going under. While they don't want to be farmers, they are just as proud of our heritage as I am. Every single one of them would be out there planting or harvesting with me if I needed it.

I give a shake of my head. "Soon. I hope to know something soon, and a lot of it has to do with the grant. Then I'll share. But until then, I don't want to get anyone excited about something that won't come to fruition."

Laken slouches slightly, a silent tell that she's not going to pump me for information. Pap just looks at me critically, and that's his tell that he's *not* going to let me go it alone at all. I bet after Laken leaves, he'll grill me hard over what's going on.

And you know what?

I'll tell him.

Everyone always spills their guts to Pap because bottom line, he usually has the best advice.

CHAPTER 3

Darby

"**M**OM... THERE'S A man over there holding a gun across his lap," Linnie says. I follow the direction of her gaze over to the hardware store.

Sure enough, a big bear of a fella sits on a rocking chair on the sidewalk with a shotgun resting across his lap. He rocks back and forth with his fingers tapping to some beat perhaps playing in his head. He's got a bushy gray beard that hangs down his chest and a pleasant smile on his face. The shotgun, however, lends an air of menace to him.

I guess that's life in a small town.

"I'm sure he's harmless," I tell her, but my hand goes to her shoulder to push her more quickly into the front door of Sweet Cakes Bakery.

The bells hanging over the door chime merrily as we enter, and a woman who I know immediately to be Larkin Mancinkus smiles at Linnie and me. I know this is Larkin Mancinkus—a.k.a. sister of Laken Mancinkus—because they're identical twins. Although Laken wears her hair long and past her shoulders, Larkin's is cut into a sweet pixie with stylishly frayed bangs that sweep across her forehead. She has a face that was meant to wear that haircut.

"You must be Darby and Linnie," Larkin says with a welcoming smile and her hands beckoning us further into the store. "Laken told me you made it into town yesterday."

My hands go to Linnie's shoulders as I smile back. "Laken told us you have the best baked goods this side of the Mississippi, so here we are."

Larkin laughs and waves the compliment off. "She's my sister. Of course she would say that."

"Well, we're here to get stocked up. I'm going to drop Linnie at Laken's veterinary clinic, and she's going to help her out for the morning while I shop for school supplies."

I don't need to look down at my daughter's face to know she's probably grimacing at the reminder I'm pawning her off on a stranger. At least that's exactly what she said to me this morning when I told her she was going to go hang out with Laken and Jake while I went shopping.

Linnie isn't bent out of shape because I'm not letting her come school shopping with me.

Quite the contrary.

I asked her to come with me, but she resoundingly turned me down. She's still in snit-mode over me making her leave Illinois, and she's taking it out on me by making it clear she doesn't want to be in my presence. I wasn't going to leave her at the farm by herself, so I gave her the choice of either coming with me to the Walmart in Milner or hanging out with Laken and Uncle Jake.

Linnie wrinkled her nose as if it was no choice at all, but grumbled she would rather spend time with Uncle Jake.

Yes, that really hurt.

I can only hope this attitude will start to mellow once she settles in. Last night, she talked to her father on the phone and he got her riled up. She had him on speakerphone as they talked, and she laid it on super thick with her dad.

"I miss you so much, Daddy," she'd told him. This was not a lie as Linnie loves her father, but I knew it was exaggerated as she never calls him "daddy". He may not be doting or overly invested in her entirety, but he is her father and there is love there.

"I really want to come home. Can I please come home and live with you?"

I gritted my teeth over her proclamation because that also hurt, but I braced myself because I knew her father's response was going to hurt her more than she had just hurt me.

"That's just not possible, Linnie," Mitch told her in a firm voice. I call it his "CEO voice" that he usually reserves for the people who work below him. "I'm just far too busy to take care of you full time. That was your mother's job, and well... she ruined that now, didn't she?"

That last line was said in the most scathing voice possible. Of course he sees it as all my fault, as he doesn't want our marriage to end and he's extremely bitter over me leaving. I guess I just can't figure out why. We didn't get along, and nothing I did seemed to please him anymore. Add on the fact he has a mistress who he kept in high style for the last two years, and I'm just not quite sure why he even cares I left. Maybe it's because I did those things he believes are the woman's role like cooking, cleaning, and raising the kids.

Might as well keep me barefoot and pregnant while he's at it.

Larkin puts her forearms on top of the glass case, which hosts an amazing variety of cakes, cookies, breads, and other pastries. She beams down at Linnie. "See anything you like? It's on the house as a welcome to Whynot."

Linnie just twists out of my hold on her shoulders and pushes past me to the door. She mutters, "Not hungry" as she jerks it open and walks out.

I watch in dismay as Linnie stomps over to a bench that

sits in front of the large glass window to the bakery. She throws herself on it and immediately slouches into a defensive posture, crossing her arms over her chest.

I rub my forehead in frustration and embarrassment before turning my weary gaze back to Larkin. "Sorry about that. I swear she's a pleasant child, but she's having the hardest time accepting this move."

Larkin waves her hand at me, brushing off my apology. "Please… kids will be kids. No need to apologize. That just means you get to have Linnie's treat."

That makes me laugh and for the first time, I have a tiny surge of happiness over the move I've made. Like validation I made the right decision.

Of course, I immediately liked Laken when I met her on my first visit several weeks ago, so it's no surprise her twin sister is just as lovely.

But Larkin has something a little bit extra in her smile I don't get from Laken. It's almost a gentle sweetness that comes from deep within her soul. I can just look at Larkin and know she's about the kindest woman I will ever meet. It's definitely in her eyes, and perhaps the fact she offered me two treats from her case.

After I pick out a chocolate croissant and a slice of banana nut bread for myself, I also order two of the jumbo chocolate chip cookies, knowing it would have been Linnie's choice. I start pointing to a variety of muffins for Jake and Laken's breakfast and as a thank-you for watching Linnie today. And without any guilt at all, I tell her to throw in a cherry pie I'll serve with dinner tonight.

As Larkin starts packaging all the treats in pretty pink boxes with cellophane windows, she chatters up a storm about the town of Whynot. I learn quickly the man on the other side of the square with the gun across his lap is Floyd. He owns the hardware store he sits in front of, and he's a self-appointed town protector even though Whynot has its own police force. She told me not to be alarmed, but Floyd often prowls around at night with his shotgun to help protect the citizens.

Luckily, I find this more charming than alarming, and it bolsters that previous surge of happiness within me. I have a feeling I'm going to like this area a lot.

"So peaches, huh?" Larkin asks as she stacks the boxes up on the counter before ringing up the purchases.

I pull my wallet out of my purse and nod. "Yeah. Peaches."

That's the main crop I'll focus on at Farrington Farms. I'm going to build Jake a peach orchard from the ground up.

"How did a woman like you get interested in agronomy?" Larkin asks me, and I realize her sister must have told her quite a bit about me since she knows my educational background.

"My sister Kelly and I grew up on a farm in Iowa," I tell her as she punches buttons on the cash register. "It was a big operation, and I was always more interested in the science behind it all."

"A smart *and* beautiful new girl in town," Larkin says with a wink. "All the boys are going to be after you before too long."

I give a humorless laugh, because having boys chase me is the last thing I want. I'm in the process of running away from a bully and would just like some peace. But sharing my history with Mitch is a little too personal right now, so I merely say, "I'm going to be far too busy getting the orchard up and running to worry about boys."

Larkin's face softens, and the empathetic look she gives

me is one of perhaps self-recognition. She gives a tiny smile and says, "Girl, I know exactly what you're talking about. Running my own business has only assured I stay single. I don't seem to have time to do anything but work and sleep."

Something in those words causes a shift within me, as if I recognize very much of myself within Larkin. Or the "self" I want to become.

Like a subtle understanding washing through me, I suddenly know Larkin and I could become very good friends. "Well, I think you and I should at least budget time to go out to lunch or something together."

Larkin grins at me. "Lunch is good. Wine and cheese one night would be better."

I grin and nod. "Much better."

I pay for the pastries minus the two Larkin gave me in welcome, and leave after exchanging phone numbers with her. We promise to try to get together within the next week.

When I step out onto the sidewalk, Linnie pretends to be engrossed in her fingernails. I hold my hand out to her. "Come on. Let's get over to Laken's clinic."

Linnie pushes up with a heavy sigh, ignores my hand, and turns toward the car. I stop her with a, "Nope. We're going to walk."

I get another overly dramatic sigh as if she'll die walking a few blocks, but I merely smile at her brightly. "It's not going to kill you."

As we walk beside each other, I make up my mind I am going to kill Linnie with kindness no matter how trying she is to me. She'll warm up to me sooner rather than later, but I would like to speed things along.

I point across the town square that's occupied by a large, red bricked courthouse. It has a beautiful lawn, grand oak trees, and a pretty, white gazebo on the southern end. "I found out the guy over there is Floyd. He's the town protector and always carries a shotgun, but I've been assured he's harmless."

She looks over to Floyd sitting in front of his hardware store but doesn't comment.

I point at the different businesses, trying to facilitate conversation. "Larkin told me this is called 'Courthouse Square'. As evidenced by the large courthouse in the town center. And that is her sister's law firm, and this bar here is owned by her grandfather."

I point out a pretty restaurant called Clementine's and tell her we need to try that. Throwing my thumb over my shoulder, I point back at an antique shop behind us. "I bet there are some cool things in there. We'll have to check all these shops out."

She doesn't respond, but I'm heartened to see her glance around with what I would deem a slight interest. We walk south along South Wright Street and then hang a left on Freemont where Laken's veterinary clinic sits one block down. She had a few appointments this morning, and I thought it would be cool for Linnie to see how a veterinarian works. It's never too early to consider career possibilities.

With some difficulty, I'm able to push open the front swinging door of Laken's clinic with my shoulder while I balance the three pink boxes on top of each other. Linnie walks in before me and comes to a dead halt. I run right into her back after I let the door close behind me, causing the boxes to tilt precariously. After I get them under control, I raise my head to see what might be the most gorgeous man I've ever seen in my entire life.

Wavy brown hair a little too long but no, on second look,

not really, and bright hazel eyes. Tanned face and cut cheekbones.

His jaw is stubbled and locked hard.

And… he's glaring at me.

CHAPTER 4

Colt

I AM ABSOLUTELY frozen in place, unable to move a muscle. Of all the negative thoughts I've had about Darby McCulhane over the last few weeks, I was not prepared to have every one of them just melt away the first time I met her because she's so beautiful.

Like she's a knockout.

A stunningly gorgeous creature.

Definitely not what I'd stereotyped a female agronomist to look like.

She has the most unusual shade of blonde hair I've ever seen.

Or is it red?

The early morning rays from the sun coming through the glass door almost make it seem as if her hair is glowing pinkish-gold. Maybe even the color of a ripe peach.

I shake my head and blink my eyes. She stares back at me with eyes the color of a glacial lake, but they aren't frosty in the slightest. Freckles are spattered over her nose and cheeks.

We just stare at each other. It's obvious she knows who I am. Just as I surely know who she is.

I had hoped to avoid this confrontation, but I had stopped by the vet clinic when I saw Laken's truck out front just to see what she was up to. She told me Darby and her daughter would be coming by this morning. The minute I heard that, I made a quick exit strategy just to avoid this very situation. I was not ready to come face to face with the woman who had become somewhat of an enemy to me even though we didn't know each other at all.

"Why are you two just staring at each other?" a small voice says, and my gaze drops to the little girl standing in front of Darby.

Laken had told me at some point in passing conversation that the kid's name was Linnie and she looks exactly like her mother. Same strawberry-gold hair, blue eyes, and freckles. Her blue eyes are magnified times ten by the thick glasses she's wearing. As if on cue, she pushes them up her nose with her index finger.

She's staring at me with open hostility, which takes me aback, but then she turns to level the same glare at her mom as she waits for an answer to her question.

Her mother doesn't answer, so I'm prompted to break the silence. "I'm Colt Mancinkus. Laken's younger brother."

My gaze goes back to Darby and I can tell by the way her eyes go round in surprise she didn't actually know who I was. Her cheeks turn red as it dawns on her I might not exactly be happy to meet her. I'm quite sure Jake filled her in on my reaction to her grant application because I sure showed my butt to him the day I confronted him about it.

Before the situation can get any more embarrassing, we're saved as Laken comes in from the back. Her voice is a combination of surprise and wariness as she takes us all in, just standing there staring at each other in silence. "Oh… Hey… I see y'all have met."

Darby seems to be frozen in place, probably feeling as uncomfortable as I do. And the best way to alleviate this awkwardness is for me to implement my original exit strategy.

I give a polite nod to Darby. When I do the same to Linnie, she just rolls her eyes at me. "It's nice to meet you both, but I've got to get going."

I start to walk past the two girls even though Laken calls behind me, "Colt. Don't go just yet."

I don't even bother to turn around and look at my sister. No way in hell I want her to facilitate some kumbaya meeting between Darby and me. I just call over my shoulder as I open the door to walk out, "Sorry, but I've got things to do. Catch y'all later."

Just before the door swings shut behind me, I think I hear Darby say something like, "Take these boxes, Linnie."

I can imagine her handing off all the Sweet Cakes boxes she had been carrying to her daughter. In my wild imagination it's so she can follow me out to talk. I make haste toward my truck, which is parallel parked in front of the clinic right behind Laken's. Escape is close as I open the driver's door, but I'm stopped by Darby's voice calling out, "Colt... can you talk for a minute?"

With a sigh, I shut the door and step back onto the sidewalk to face Darby. I grimace over the fact she looks even more beautiful in the sunlight, and I don't want to have any positive feelings toward this woman right now. It's easier to be mired in the negativity.

Still, I manage to put a bland yet polite smile on my face. "What's up?"

She studies me for a moment as if trying to figure out the best approach to take. Darby doesn't know me at all, only that I'm not happy she applied for the grant. She also knows her family and mine may ultimately be merged at some point if Laken and Jake were to get married. This makes things a little sticky between us.

Finally, she says, "I know you're angry with me. And I'm sorry for that. Had I known you before I applied for that grant, things might have been different."

I can't help raising a skeptical eyebrow. "So now that you know who I am and how important this grant is to my family, are you going to withdraw your application?"

This takes her by surprise. She blinks repeatedly at me while her mouth opens and closes as she tries to answer. I put her on the spot, but I'm genuinely curious as to what her position might now be.

I'm slightly disappointed when she says, "I don't know. I still don't know you and why the grant is so important. But I need you to know it's important to me as well."

I can't help but scoff. "Yes, because you need to write a paper about it. I'm sure you must be in a very dire situation."

She narrows those beautiful eyes at me, which are now very, very frosty. "It may not be dire, but it goes directly to my livelihood. I need this degree in order to provide a good life for my daughter and me."

I wish she wouldn't have brought her kid into it because that is actually something that would pull at my heartstrings if I let it. I've got to stay focused, though, on the fact my family and our farm is more important than any need that she may have. Before I can tell her that, she asks me, "What exactly would you use the grant for?"

I wasn't prepared for this question, and I haven't discussed my plans for a winery with anyone. I think the fear of failure has me hesitant to even voice my plans out loud. Ridiculous, I know, but there it is.

I start to tell her it's none of her business, but she steps in closer and lowers her voice. Putting a hand on my arm, she says, "I'd be glad to help you with whatever project you have."

There's no stopping the sarcastic bubble of a laugh that wells up. "And just how much farming experience do you have?"

I know the answer to this already as Laken had told me enough about Darby McCulhane. She grew up on a commercial farm, which was mostly mechanized production. I doubt she's ever put her hands in the dirt before.

My surly attitude is not appreciated. Her hand drops from my arm, and she takes a step back while lifting her chin in an aloof manner. She doesn't reply to my question. "Well, whatever it is you're doing, I wish you the best of luck. And I wish you luck on the grant as well."

My jaw locks tight. I can't wish her luck back because I might jinx myself and not get the grant. And that would be unthinkable.

Darby stares at me for a moment. When she realizes I'm not going to wish her luck back, she understands I'm being a complete jackass. She gives me a curt nod before turning on her heel. A strange sensation bubbles up within me, and I realize I'm being swamped with regret over my manners. My mother raised me better than this. Before I can stop myself, I'm calling out, "I'm sorry. I don't mean to be such a jerk about this."

Darby whips around to face me, her face awash with surprise, but hesitant to believe my words.

I take a step toward her, shoving my hands into the pockets of my jeans. "I just take all of this very personally since it's my family's livelihood and has been that way for eight generations."

Darby's eyebrows raise upward, and she whistles through her teeth. "Eight generations?"

I nod with a smile. "We were deeded the land from the

King of England."

Darby steps in and tilts her head, lifting her chin slightly. "Seriously… what are you going to use the grant for?"

My eyes cut over to the clinic door as if I expect Laken to be leaning out and eavesdropping. I don't see her, so I turn back to Darby and decide to let her in on it. "I'd like to plant grapes. I want to open a winery on Mainer Farms."

There is no mistaking the look of respect on Darby's face. "Now that sounds like a cool plan. Have you ever grown grapes before?"

I give a shake of my head. "I've done a lot of research, and I talked to a man who owns a winery a couple of counties over yesterday. I feel confident I can do it."

Darby nods in what seems to be agreement in my abilities even though she doesn't know me from Adam. "Well, I'd be glad to talk about the sciences behind it anytime you want. I've actually got a good friend I completed my master's program with who works at a vineyard out in California if you want me to put you in touch with him."

This is all kind of weird. Ten minutes ago, this woman was as close to a mortal enemy as I had, and now she's offering me help on starting a vineyard. Well, not to help but at least to advise. Proves to me Darby McCulhane is good people despite my initial perception about her.

Beautiful and good people. Quite the combination, and it means I can't stay mad at her.

CHAPTER 5

Darby

I DO A slow pace up and down the heavily scuffed tile floor in the Department of Agriculture building. I received a surprising and unexpected phone call two days ago that the expansion grant board had a tough time deciding between my application and Colt's. They asked me to come to Raleigh for a formal interview. While I have not seen or talked to Colt since our first meeting four days ago, I can only assume he received the same request.

I'm not pacing because I'm nervous. It's just how I've always been... unable to sit still for any length of time. I'm not in the slightest bit worried about this grant because Jake doesn't actually need it. When I boil it all down, the application process is what's most important to my thesis.

The door to the boardroom where I was instructed to be at ten o'clock this morning opens, and I turn to face whoever may be coming out. I have no clue who's going to be interviewing me today—whether it's one person or several. Clasping my hands placidly in front of me, I put a confident smile on my face.

To my surprise, Colt Mancinkus steps out of the boardroom. The minute his eyes land on me, an easy smile comes to his face.

He pulls the door shut behind him and says, "I take it they're interviewing you next?"

My return smile is just as easy. "And I take it you just had your interview."

Colt takes a few steps toward me and lowers his voice as if to conspire. "It was a piece of cake."

I lean in toward him and give a mischievous wink. "Well then, perhaps you'll share some pointers with me."

Colt lets out a deep, rich laugh of amusement. It makes his eyes crinkle slightly at the corners as they sparkle with brilliance. Frankly, it amps up his hotness factor. "Not about to give you any help for this grant, Miss McCulhane."

I didn't expect him to give me any help, and it's all in good fun right now. While we're both chuckling, I take a moment to really look at Colt. He's wearing a pair of faded jeans and a gray and red plaid flannel shirt. He's got on cowboy boots and a thick brown leather belt with a large silver belt buckle. The only thing missing that would make him look more cowboy than farmer is a cowboy hat, but it would be a travesty to cover up that thick, wavy hair.

I compare his attire to mine, and I realize I've made a very crucial mistake in this interview already. Colt looks every bit like a farmer from North Carolina. I'm wearing a black business pantsuit with four-inch stiletto heels and a cream silk blouse under my jacket. I look like I'm ready to attend a banker's meeting or something, and I know deep within my heart I've put myself at a disadvantage dressing this way.

To my surprise, Colt gives a nod to the boardroom and says, "There are four board members in there. They're all nice, and my interview took about fifteen minutes. They're just going to ask you the reason for the application and some more details about how you intend to use it. Nothing you can't handle."

My chin pulls in as I blink at Colt's magnanimous gift of

information. "Thank you. That wasn't necessary, but thank you."

Colt just shrugs and puts one hand in his pocket. "I figure what will be will be. It does no good to worry about it. As my pap told me yesterday, all I can do is try my best."

"Now that sounds like some great advice," I tell him. "And I need to get by Chesty's to meet your grandpa. Laken and Jake have told me a lot about him."

Colt nods and smiles in a way that makes my belly flutter a little. "Come on by Saturday if you want. I'll be working and will gladly buy you a beer."

"You work at Chesty's?"

"It's a long story, but the condensed version is I need the money," Colt tells me without an ounce of bitterness or hardship in his voice. More like steely determination, and that intrigues me. "I'll fill you in over a beer. Promise."

"Sounds like a plan."

The boardroom door opens once again, and we turn to look that way. A middle-aged woman with a blonde bob peeks out, her eyes first going to Colt and then to me. "Miss McCulhane?"

"That's me," I tell her pleasantly. I grab my purse from the bench where I had set it earlier. Hitching it over my shoulder, I walk toward the woman.

"Knock 'em dead," Colt calls out. I level a grin back at him over my shoulder, marveling how we have suddenly become friends even though we're both competing for the same grant and Colt was pretty bent out of shape about it.

I'm a little flustered as I walk into the boardroom, again not because I'm nervous about this interview but because that short conversation with Colt has thrown me off a little. There's no doubt Colt was being all neighborly just now, but there's also no doubt we were flirting a little bit. This is confusing to me as flirting is probably the last thing in the world I want to do with the man. And yet, it had just come out of me so naturally.

I give a small shake of my head, and walk down to the end of a long conference room table where the blonde woman points. After I take a seat, they introduce themselves. I nod with a polite smile to each of them.

Then the questions begin. They spend a few minutes going over some of the details in my application, focusing in on the fact I intend to split the orchard into three parts and use different applications of micronutrients, so I can figure out the best method to increase the yield and quality. I can tell my scientific approach is intriguing to them.

"And what exactly is your experience with farming?" one of the board members asks me; a tall, thin man with slicked-back gray hair and a tan, weathered face. I imagine he farmed for many years before becoming a board member at the Department of Agriculture.

I give a little cough to clear my throat, putting my hands on the conference room table where I clasp them loosely. "I grew up on a large farm in Iowa. We mostly produced corn but also some wheat and soybeans. My bachelor and master's degrees are in agronomy, and I'm in the process of completing my PhD in the same field."

The board members nod and jot down some notes.

The blonde woman, who introduced herself as Belinda Caldwell, gives me a challenging look. "Does this grant, and the planned peach orchard, have anything to do with you getting your PhD?"

I'm nodding in full disclosure before she even finishes her question. "I'm focusing part of my thesis on the orchard. The grant application will also be a part of it."

Miss Caldwell nods, jots something down, and looks back to me. "And what are your plans after you get your degree? Or after you get the orchard planted?"

"I intend to stay at Farrington Farms for several months after the planting. But I'm also going to apply to some companies that specialize in crop sciences. There are several good ones right here in Research Triangle Park, but I would be applying to some in other states as well."

They asked this question because they want to get an idea of my commitment to the project, so I add on, "Before I leave, though, I would oversee hiring an operations manager to take my place in managing the orchard. It is a long-term project for Farrington Farms that we do not intend to give up."

One of the other board members gives a slight cough to grab my attention. When I cut my eyes his way, he asks, "Why is your project for the peach orchard more important to the community than Mr. Mancinkus' project to open a vineyard on Mainer Farms?"

This question does catch me by surprise because it has nothing to do with how the grant should be awarded. And I cannot even think to lie, but give them the most honest answer I can. "I don't believe the peach orchard is more important to the community than the vineyard. If you are going strictly by community standards, I believe the Mainer Farms' grant application should be given a higher considera-tion than mine. I understand they've been farming the land for eight generations, and I've been living in Whynot, North Carolina for all of two weeks. I have no standing in this community. My commitment is only but words I can give you. Mainer Farms has real history, and I expect it has a direct impact on the economy in the area."

Miss Caldwell blinks at me in surprise. She tilts her head and says, "I have to tell you, Miss McCulhane, you were actually our top contender coming into this interview process. You sure you want to stick to that answer?"

I don't even spare a moment to consider the consequences. "I'm going to stick to my answer."

All the board members start furiously jotting down notes. And I realize I've thrown them for a loop as they truly were more interested in my orchard project than the vineyard. And I also realize this isn't just about the importance to Colt and his family, but perhaps to the community as a whole. I may not have been living here long, but what little bit I've come to know I really respect.

"In fact," I say carefully as all sets of eyes come to me. "Is it possible for me to withdraw my application?"

It feels like the air is sucked out of the room and the board members look at me in bewilderment. Miss Caldwell gives me a tight smile. "That is your choice, of course, though I'm not sure I would recommend it."

I push up from my chair and place the palms of my hands on the tabletop. Glancing around the room, I give each board member an appreciative smile. "I really, really appreciate all of you taking the time to consider my request. But it suddenly occurred to me there could be other factors that are more important than my needs for that grant. I know of no industry that has such an important sense of community than farming, and your question prompted me to consider that. I'm going to formally withdraw my application, and it is my sincere hope you will have no qualms in giving the grant to Mainer Farms."

Miss Caldwell throws her pen down onto her notepad with a huff, but the other board members smile at me with respect.

All I know is that when I pull away from the Department of Agriculture building, I'm feeling very good about my decision.

CHAPTER 6

Colt

SATURDAY NIGHT IS the busiest time of the week at Chesty's. The crowd is always a mix of varying ages but locals to the area. Saturday night is also when the real drinkers come out to Chesty's. The regulars include Judge Bowe, who is standing next to Pap's bar stool drinking a draft beer; Floyd, who is nursing a Coca-Cola because he'll be on town protection duty later tonight with his shotgun; and Billy Crump from the grocery store. I also see Jason Miller and Della Padgett, who are dating and will often come in for an early drink on Saturday.

The one person who is noticeably absent from the seat next to Pap is my sister, Trixie. Before she reconnected with her first love, Ry Powers, Trixie was here every Saturday night with Pap. Those two are tighter than tight. While she may not hang out with him at Chesty's as much as she did before, she is still the apple of his eye over the rest of us Mancinkus kids.

"Colt… can I get two Bud Lights and a Michelob," someone hollers from the opposite end of the bar from where Pap and Judge Bowe are standing. I turn that way to see Gill Ellis standing with his crony Travis Robbins, and Travis' girlfriend, Cindy Lou Peep. Not kidding about that name. It's really Cindy Lou Peep.

I withhold a grimace because Gill and Travis are two of the biggest redneck jerks in Scuppernong County. They've been run out of Pap's bar more times than not. It wasn't overly long ago they were banned for saying horrible things to a good friend of the Mancinkus clan. Morri D is quite the character. Black, gay, and a cross-dresser on occasion, he's the best friend of my brother Lowe's wife, Mely. That makes Morri one of us, and we don't let people mess around with family or friends of family. Their racist, homophobic comments earned them a one-way ticket out to the sidewalk.

I heard through the grapevine that Gill and Travis came to Pap with their tails between their legs and thoroughly apologized for their behavior. Pap wasn't having any of it. He told them they couldn't come back into the bar until they apologized to Morri himself. Since Morri was back in New York, this presented a problem for the dudes.

But their love of drinking beer and playing pool in Chesty's outweighed the difficulties they faced. They begged Mely and Lowe for Morri's phone number, then they called him and apologized. Pap verified.

I don't feel for a second it was genuine. It only served their purpose to be allowed back in Chesty's, but a deal's a deal. It will merely be any given night coming up in the future they'll do something stupid and get kicked out again. Until then, they're paying customers.

I grab the beers they requested, twisting the tops off and flicking them expertly into the large garbage can that sits underneath the cash register. After I make change for the purchases, I notice the door opening and my heart skips a tiny beat when Darby walks in behind my sister, Larkin. I don't spare but a glance at my sister and instead, I focus on the beautiful blonde I'm embarrassed to say I have thought about a time or two this past week.

When I saw her two days ago at the Department of Agriculture, she was dressed as an elegantly chic businesswoman. Tonight, she looks like she belongs in Whynot, wearing well-fitted jeans and a plain, but pretty, black sweater that hangs off one shoulder. My eyes travel down the length of her, and I smile when I see she's wearing a pair of black Chuck Taylor's.

As if she knew I was staring at her, Darby's eyes immediately catch mine as I wipe down the bar top. Larkin grabs her hand, taking her attention and leading her over to where Pap is. I cut my eyes over there often, watching as Larkin introduces Darby first to Pap, who gives her a hearty handshake, and next to Judge Bowe, who inclines his head to her in a southern gentleman fashion. Pap barks at two customers who are sitting on the barstools next to him, and they jump up to offer Darby and Larkin their seats.

That's my cue to walk that way and take their order.

I ignore Travis Robbins as he calls out to me for something else, knowing he's not going anywhere and I will get whatever he wants later. Using my wet rag to wipe down the area right in front of where Darby and Larkin are sitting, I give my most genial and charming smile to Darby as I ask, "What are you drinking tonight, darlin'?"

Larkin rolls her eyes so dramatically I can actually see it out of my peripheral vision. She answers for them both. "Give us two drafts."

I don't even look at my sister but instead wink at Darby. "Coming right up."

When I bring the two frosty mugs filled with ice-cold beer to the ladies, I tell Darby, "That's on me tonight."

She blushes prettily and inclines her head. "Thank you very much."

"My pleasure."

She takes a sip of the beer and sets the mug back down on

the counter top. After swallowing, she gives me a pointed look and says, "I understand congratulations are in order."

I lean over, placing an elbow on the bar top so I don't have to yell above the music and chatter of the patrons. I had been expecting her to say something like that since I had gotten notice this morning via a telephone call I had been awarded the expansion granted by the Department of Agriculture. Darby would have gotten a call as well to let her know she did not get it.

"I will take your congratulations but I'm the one that needs to be thanking you," I tell her with a solemn look.

She looks confused, but I'm not buying it for a moment. I lean in even closer. "I know you pulled your application."

Darby's chin jerks inward, and she tries to pull off an even more surprised yet slightly affronted expression. "Why would you ever think that?"

I chuckle and lean in just a little bit closer to her. Her blue eyes are absolutely mesmerizing. "Darlin'… there's a little thing around here called the gossip mill. You probably don't have one of these where you're from but let me tell you, it means you can't hide anything around here."

"Gossip mill?" A strawberry-blonde eyebrow arches high.

I nod effusively. "Gossip mill. You see, Donnie Rhodes is one of the gentleman who was on the board interviewing us two days ago. His wife Linda has a cousin, Trudy, who lives here in Whynot. She was apparently in Central Café yesterday telling Floyd all about the interviews and how you told the board the grant should be awarded to Mainer Farms. Furthermore, my understanding is that when one of the board members indicated you might be in the lead for votes, you actually requested your application be withdrawn."

I give her a satisfied smirk and cut my eyes toward Larkin.

She's highly entertained by this conversation.

When I turn back to Darby, she is lowering her eyes somewhat shyly down to her beer.

"Seriously, though, Darby. Thank you." I stare until she lifts her gaze to mine and gives a small nod of acknowledgment of my gratitude.

"Therefore, all of your beers for the rest of your life here in Chesty's are on me."

Travis Robbins yells from the other end of the bar again. "Colt. The jukebox took my money, dammit."

Before Darby can say anything else, I give her a wink and push off from the counter. "Duty calls."

♦

IT ONLY GETS busier as the night wears on, and I find myself with little opportunity to socialize with anyone. I'm hopping from customer to customer, filling beer orders and the occasional glass of wine. The more people drink, the more I cook my share of frozen pizzas. The food at Chesty's is basic. Frozen pizza, which is best served with Texas Pete hot sauce and garlic salt, a variety of chips or peanuts, and a large jar of pickled eggs and beets that Pap makes himself every week. Sounds disgusting, but they're actually really good.

I can't help but notice Darby seems to be having a good time. She's a beer drinker… Corona to be exact. She switched over after the first draft beer, and I diligently bought them for her all night. She didn't seem to mind Chesty's isn't fancy enough to carry lime wedges. She and Larkin bounce around the bar playing pool or darts. In between those games, they come back to sit next to Pap, carrying on lively conversations. It also doesn't slip my notice that several of the male patrons attempt to flirt with Darby. She rebuffs all of them politely, and I'm not sure how that makes me feel. I would bet she's still too fresh off her marriage ending to even give another man attention in the romantic way.

"Colt," Pap calls me, and I walk his way.

"What's up?" I ask. He doesn't want a beer because the one in front of him is half full.

"Why don't you take a break?" he says as he pushes off his barstool. "I'll watch the bar for about fifteen or twenty minutes."

I cock an eyebrow at Pap. In all the years I have been bartending for him, he has never once offered to watch the bar for me so I can take a break. I don't point this out, but instead say, "You know you can't be behind the bar because you've been drinking."

"I'm as sober as one of the Whynot church ladies on Sunday morning," he retorts.

This is untrue. He is not sober, but he also isn't drunk. He never gets drunk. He'll usually just nurse a few beers through the night. Still, that's not my point. "It doesn't matter if you're drunk or not; the law says you can't be behind the bar drinking."

"I won't be drinking," he says with a sly grin. "I'll just be manning the bar while you take a little break."

I put my elbows on the bar top and lean toward him. "What are you doing?"

"Not doing anything," he says evasively.

He's up to something, but I don't feel like figuring it out right this second. He's offering me a break, and I'm not one to turn my nose up at that. I gallantly push open the swing-through door at the end of the bar and make a dramatic sweeping motion with my arm for him to come back into my inner sanctum. He snorts at my antics, grumbling something about me not being too old to take over his knee as he brushes past me.

I slip through the door to the other side of the bar and take the seat he had just vacated. I call out after him, "Hey… bring me a beer, why don't you?"

Whether he hears me, I don't know because my attention is taken by two hands clapping down on my shoulders. I turn to find Larkin standing there with a sloppy grin on her face. She's on her way to getting drunk.

"What are you doing on this side of the bar?" she says. She proceeds to wrap her arms around my neck to give me a stranglehold of a hug.

I pull her arms away from my neck. "Pap insisted I take a break."

Larkin moves from my back to my side, cocking an identical eyebrow to the one I threw at Pap moments ago. "He's up to something."

I chuckle and nod in agreement. "Totally up to something."

At that moment, Darby plops down in the stool adjacent to mine and gives an overly dramatic huff of fatigue. "That's it. I'm done. No more darts because I suck."

"You don't suck," Larkin says, and I can tell this has been a subject of debate between them tonight. "You just need some practice."

Darby shakes her head, causing her unusually colored locks to swirl around her shoulders. I have to resist the urge to reach out and touch it.

"I'm not meant to be a dart player," she laments. "Or a pool player. If I come to a bar, what I'm good at is drinking beer, and I think I'll stick to that."

That makes me laugh and it's as if Darby didn't realize I

was sitting there, because she brings her eyes to mine.

"Well hello there, Colt Mancinkus," she says with a toothy grin.

"Hello there, Darby McCulhane," I reply with a corresponding playful smile. "I'm thinking you girls are going to need a ride home tonight. If you stay until I close the bar, I'll take you both home."

Larkin reaches an arm between Darby and me to grab her beer off the bar top. She tilts it back and drains it. "I'll probably be passed out before the bar closes. I'm sure Andy will give us a ride home soon."

Andy Forrester is one of the town deputies. If he's on duty tonight, he'll gladly give Larkin and Darby a ride home. He's been sweet on Larkin since we were in grade school, but I know the sentiment is not returned on her part. She's kept him totally in the friend zone for years.

"How are you settling in?" I ask Darby.

Darby smiles and gives me a hapless shrug. "I'm loving it here. It's so quiet and peaceful, and I don't have to deal with…"

Her words trail off. It's clear she's avoiding a touchy subject, which I am assuming is her husband.

"Where is Linnie tonight?" I ask to change the subject. I'm gallant that way.

Darby's face pinches, and she wrinkles her nose slightly before she answers, "Her father made a surprise trip to North Carolina this weekend. She's staying the night with him."

I have no clue what the deal is between Darby and her soon-to-be ex-husband. The most Laken has told me is it was not a good marriage, and it was Darby's decision to leave. It's also really none of my business so I don't ask her about it.

Before I can change the subject once again, Larkin grabs

Darby and pulls her from the stool. "Come on… Let's go play one more game of pool."

Darby rolls her eyes. Laughing, she gives me an exasperated grin as she allows my sister to lead her off.

I watch both women for a few minutes, pondering the mystery of Darby McCulhane. She is nothing like I expected. I have to admit I'm greatly intrigued by her.

CHAPTER 7

Darby

I HEAR THE crunch of gravel outside and peek through the lacy curtains covering the kitchen window above the sink. As expected, Mitch's rental car is coming up the long gravel driveway to Farrington Farms. Even though I've escaped what had become an intolerable situation with Mitch over the last few years, my skin still crawls with the prospect of having to deal with him. It was an extremely difficult decision to leave him, and a brutal experience breaking the news to him that I wanted out of the marriage.

Mitch has been nothing but combative, manipulative, and determined not to let me get away. When he showed up at the farm on Friday night without even bothering to give me a head's-up he was coming to North Carolina, there was a part of me that was a little fearful. Almost as if I were being stalked, but I told myself it was ridiculous. Mitch was here for Linnie.

Or so he said.

As it turns out, Mitch—if he can be believed—had a meeting at his company's office in Raleigh. It was not unusual for him to travel at least once a quarter to North Carolina, so I can't say for sure whether this was a legitimate trip. I don't think for a moment his main goal in coming out to the farm was to see Linnie as he suggested, but rather to put himself in my presence and make yet another appeal for us to come back home.

I'm proud I shut him down fairly quickly on Friday, and I had absolutely no problem bundling up Linnie with a small bag of essentials for her to stay with him for two nights at a hotel in Raleigh. While her sulking had diminished somewhat, I was still getting plenty of attitude from her. I'd hoped spending two days with her father might remind her I was actually the fun, loving, and genuinely caring parent out of the two of us.

Mitch pulls the car parallel with the sprawling porch that runs along the front of the house and continues in an L-shape around the eastern side of the structure. There's nothing on the porch, but I imagine it would look beautiful with some rocking chairs and potted ferns hanging from above.

I dry my hands on a dish towel and make my way out onto the front porch, resting my hands on my hips as Mitch and Linnie get out of the car. He pulls her backpack out of the backseat and hands it to her.

"Why don't you take this inside?" he instructs her.

Linnie stares at him a moment, probably not sure if this is where she should hug him goodbye or not. Mitch doesn't help her out at all, only adding, "I need to talk to your mother."

He reaches out and ruffles her hair, and I can see this confuses her even more. Knowing Mitch, this is his goodbye to his daughter. I'm not sure he would even think to bend over to give her something as parental as a hug or tell her how much he's going to miss her.

Linnie takes the backpack and without a word to her father, she heads up the porch steps. I give her an encouraging smile, but she won't meet my eyes, so I reach out and stop her with my arm across her chest. She actually lets me pull her into my side and, amazingly, also lets me kiss the top of her head. "Missed you, kiddo."

"Missed you too," she mumbles before walking into the house. I watch her until the swinging screen door claps shut and then brace myself as I turn to face Mitch.

He doesn't come up the porch steps, but casually tucks his hands into a pair of pressed khaki pants he paired with a white golf shirt. He looks at me expectantly, as if I'm the one who wants to talk to him rather than the other way around.

I merely cross my arms over my chest and wait him out.

"Have you given any more thought to coming home?" he asks me in a brittle voice.

I study my husband critically, not moved in the slightest by his charming good looks that have only gotten better as he's aged. I met Mitch when I was twenty-one and fresh out of college. I had decided to work for John Deere to get some experience on the business of farming and to help pay my way through my master's and PhD programs. Mitch was thirty-three and already a young executive with the company at their main headquarters in Moline, Illinois. The eleven-year age difference didn't bother me in the slightest and in hindsight, I think Mitch liked the idea I was so much younger than he was. At first, I thought maybe it was just for bragging rights, having a young pretty wife, but I came to realize soon enough he used my age and perhaps my immaturity to manipulate me into doing things the way he wanted. Let's face it. I had stars in my eyes and loved him so much he didn't have to do much manipulating at first.

I give a silent sigh, refusing to let Mitch know his words bother me. "I'm not going to change my mind, Mitch. This is permanent."

He lets out a bark of disbelief and throws his hands out wide. His voice is scathing when he asks, "You're seriously going to live here in the middle of nowhere? And work on a farm? You're seriously okay with giving up the lifestyle I gave you, along with our circle of friends?"

My eyes narrow as I look down from the porch at my husband. "Yes, Mitch. I'm completely fine with giving all that up. It's not what I ever wanted in life to begin with."

His disbelieving snort matches the roll of his eyes. "Yes, I know. Your degree is more important than your family."

This infuriates me because it's not true in the slightest, and he's absolutely mischaracterizing why I'm here in North Carolina to begin with.

I stomp down the porch steps until I come toe to toe with him. "Your concept of family and my concept of family are two totally different things. Everything I'm doing now is for Linnie, not myself. I'm getting a degree, so I can support my daughter and myself without needing to rely on anyone else. And Mitch… You and I as a couple stopped being a part of the family component years ago. If you need any further reminder of why that's true, it's because you've been paying for a mistress for two years behind my back. So get off your high and mighty soapbox and get it through your head that I am done with this marriage."

This takes Mitch aback because I rarely fight with him. He pulls his chin in and blinks in surprise. His slightly reddened cheeks are the only indication the mistress thing bothers him. "I told you I would get rid of her."

I try not to laugh. Try really hard. But I find it comical Mitch still hasn't ended the affair with that woman. He's holding her in reserve in case he can't talk me into coming back.

When my laugh does come out, it's bitter and my voice is sad for everything I've lost over the years. "Mitch… hear me out. Our marriage didn't crumble because you had a mistress. Me finding out about her was merely the catalyst that gave me the strength to end this. But I wanted out for a lot longer. I wanted out for years and it's because you kept me so under your thumb and wouldn't let me pursue my dreams. Now that I want to do that, it's unfathomable to you that I could want something other than the things you've given me or the things you've told me to do. What I really need you to hear is that I'm doing this for Linnie and not to hurt you. I'm doing it so she grows up to be the type of woman who goes for what she wants. If she watches me continue to give up my life day in and day out to please you, I'm not teaching her right."

I suck in a deep breath and let it out slowly. That was the first time I've been so brutally honest with Mitch. It's the first time I've been able to get out the words I hope will make him understand he and I are just never going to work. I had hoped he might actually listen to me. That he might put himself in my shoes and try to see things from my point of view.

But this is Mitch McCulhane. A man whose ego is so overinflated, he can't seem to understand that other people may have valid opinions, wants, or desires from his own.

He doesn't look at me with the understanding I had so foolishly hoped for, and not even a bit of sadness for what we've lost. Flames leap in his eyes and his jaw locks tight. He grits through his teeth, "You are making a serious mistake. I am gravely concerned about the welfare of our daughter. I might just have to go back and get my attorney to start working on custody of Linnie."

A small jolt of fear punches through me. Linnie is my weakness and if there is any possibility he could get full custody of her, I'd prostrate myself in front of him in deference.

But the one thing I have to keep my mind focused on is I know my husband. Mitch would never want full custody of his daughter. Hell, I don't think he wants partial custody of her. From the day we brought her home from the hospital, he treated Linnie like a pretty object to show off to other people. He never fed her, diapered her, or sang her lullabies before bed. In Mitch's mind, that was my role as her mother. I did them, of course, because I loved doing them. Loved every minute I spent with my daughter.

Mitch didn't do anything because he was always working. He justified his absence in her life as a necessity to give her the finer things. In other words, he tried to buy her love the way he tried to buy mine. He never went to spelling bees or to watch her show her horse. He never asked her how school was going or sat down to read her a book. He was the provider. He worked hard to give us a good life. In Mitch's mind, that should have been enough.

It was never enough for me, and I know damn well it's not enough for Linnie.

I shore up my spine and lift my chin with resolve.

"You do that if you need to, Mitch," I say in a soft voice that is no less diminished with surety in what I'm saying. "But you and I both know you're not going to do it. You don't have it in you to be a single father. You would never want a child to cramp your lifestyle."

Mitch's face turns redder, and I notice him clenching his fists tightly. While Mitch has been a manipulative and verbally abusive husband over the years, he has never once raised his hands to me. But for a moment, I see something within his eyes that tells me he may have the capacity for violence. It turns my blood ice cold, and it takes everything within me not to run away in fear. I can't show him that because Mitch would pounce.

"This isn't over, Darby," Mitch says in a low, menacing voice.

I don't reply because any words that would come out of my mouth would be shaky and warbled because his last words really rattled me. He's making it clear I am still very much considered his property and nothing I say matters to him.

I stand silently as Mitch spins on his heel and stomps around to the driver's side door. I don't move from my spot until he has turned out of the driveway onto the highway and disappeared.

After letting out a long breath of relief, I take note of a low-level headache that is now throbbing behind my eyes. With the promise of a few Excedrin on the horizon, I turn back toward the porch, but immediately come to a stop again.

Linnie is standing there and I have no clue how long she had been listening to her father and me. She's got a funny look on her face I could not begin in a million years to decipher. She's seven going on fifteen, and she has been through great emotional upheaval the last few months. Linnie is as apt to yell at me as she would be to hug me.

So I wait—standing absolutely still—to see what she's going to do.

"Am I going to have to go live with Dad if he gets custody of me?" she asks timidly, as if the fear in her voice discounts all the crap she's given me for taking her away from him over the last week.

"I don't know, honey," I tell her honestly. "Do you want to go live with him?"

Linnie shakes her head, which causes the braided pigtails she had over each shoulder to fly back. She pushes her glasses up her nose. "No. He really didn't want to spend time with me this weekend. All he did was work in the hotel room. I just watched TV."

What a jerk, but totally not surprising.

"I know you're having a hard time adjusting, Linnie. All I can tell you is it will get better over time."

Linnie doesn't answer me, but she also doesn't glare at me. This is a good sign.

It's a miracle when I get a small smile before she asks, "What's for dinner?"

I was going to make a pork roast, but I make a spur-of-the-moment change. "You're favorite—spaghetti."

Her smile gets bigger, and I'm pretty sure everything is going to be fine between us.

CHAPTER 8

Colt

EVERY SUNDAY FOR as long as I can remember, my mama, Catherine Mancinkus, has cooked a large family meal that was served promptly at two PM. This gave her the opportunity to attend Sunday church services with plenty of time left to come home to make a feast fit for a king. There were always the usual staples of a southern Sunday dinner. Biscuits or cornbread, sweet tea, and a homemade dessert. We would also have ham, meatloaf, or country-fried steak. There were always classic sides like collards, macaroni and cheese, or butter beans.

When I was around six, Pap came to live full time in North Carolina from Pittsburgh. Ever since his move here, our Sunday dinner got supplemented with some of his favorites he grew up with in his Polish/Lithuanian family. That meant there was usually halupki or sauerkraut served. Sometimes Mama would make pierogis.

Us Mancinkus kids loved it. We considered these additions to Sunday dinner to be exotic, sort of how we viewed our eccentric grandfather from up North. Pap, on the other hand, became enamored of southern cooking and was completely fine with ham, collards, and cornbread for dinner. He was willing to give up his northern-rooted food. However, we were not since we had come to love it, so my mama had a very eclectic selection of food on Sunday.

Today the Mancinkus dining room is filled to capacity. My dad, Jerry, sits on one end of the long table, and Pap sits on the other. My mother sits to the left of my dad, followed by Trixie, her fiancé Ry, and then Laken, who is looking morose over the fact Jake could not be here since he's in California on business.

On my side of the table, Lowe sits to my right with his wife Mely beside him and Larkin on the other side. There's no conversation going on in this exact moment because we're all too busy passing bowls around the table, counterclockwise as is our tradition. I take a large scoop of red beans and rice from a white ceramic bowl before passing it to Lowe. My hands are immediately filled with a platter of jalapeno cornbread. I take two slices.

"When are you going to fill us in about the grant you got awarded?" Pap says from my right.

I throw him a smirking glance, because he likes to stir stuff up. But the joke is on him. I had intended to lay out my plans for the vineyard tonight to the entire family.

Handing the cornbread off to Lowe, I take a sip of my sweet tea before I answer. I take a moment to glance around the table and see that everyone's attention is on me with keen interest, as evidenced by the fact they're all ignoring the delicious food before them.

I decide to do them a favor and make it short. "I'm going to plant grapes on the western side of the farm. Some muscadine but also some vinifera grapes. And then I'm going to make wine from them."

Once again, I look around the table. Dad, Laken, and Larkin have their mouths open in surprise. My mom stares at me with pride. I glance to my right and see Lowe is nodding—perhaps tacit approval without hearing more—and

Mely has an expression on her face that seems to say she can't determine whether this is a good idea.

It's Pap who asks the first question. "What's your game plan?"

Nice. Simple. Nonjudgmental. Pap's got it going on tonight.

"I had to write up a five-year business plan when I submitted for the expansion grants. Anyone of y'all can take a look at it if you want. The short story, though, is it's going to take two to three years for the vines to produce. Another year after that to get the wine production settled. I'm hoping by the fifth year I'll be able to break even, and we can start making a profit after that. Assuming our wine tastes good enough to sell."

"You're going to give up some of the leased land?" my dad asks. There's a tiny bit of doubt in his voice, but that's understandable. He hasn't been working morning, noon, and night on this project the way I have for the last few years, so he doesn't know the ins and outs the way I do. He's also been removed from the business of our current operations, preferring to do semi-retired tinkering around the farm as is his due.

I nod. "The expansion grant will cover some of that lost revenue, but I have enough repeat buyers for our cattle I've been gradually expanding over the last few years that it will compensate."

And that's all my dad needs to know. He and my mom put me in charge of Mainer Farms, and I've been running it solidly for the last few years. We've been struggling, but that's mainly due to our inability to maintain our tobacco crops. Imported tobacco is just way too cheap for a smaller farm like us to compete with, so we've had to get creative and find other avenues to keep the farm going. While the easy fix was to lease out land, by doing the cattle and now the vineyard, I'm hoping we can become a fully self-sustaining farm once again.

"I think it sounds like an amazing idea," Mely says from the other side of Lowe, leaning forward to look past him to me. I shoot her a grateful smile in return before she says, "You realize you could actually use tourism as an income earner once you get up and running. You could open up a restaurant and have wine tastings."

Chuckling, I give her another nod. "It's something I would like to research, but that might be about ten years down the road."

"What do you need from us, honey?" my mom asks.

My answer to her is simple. "Just your support."

"You always have that," she says, and then my cheeks turn hot when she continues, "We are so proud of what you've done with the farm. We believe you can accomplish anything."

"Amen to that," Larkin says.

And to my surprise, Laken holds up her glass of sweet tea. "To my brother, Colt Mancinkus. The finest farmer these parts has ever seen."

Everyone follows suit and picks up their glasses, raising them high. They all say things such as, "here, here" or "to Colt".

"We need to spike this sweet tea with some peach moonshine," Pap says, and everyone laughs.

But not for long as my mom gets up and goes into the kitchen, reaching into a back cabinet where she keeps some of Billy Crump's mason jars filled with his specialty peach moonshine.

This has turned into a good day. I generally expected my

family to be supportive. Like I've always said, there's not one of them sitting at this table who wouldn't give their own skin for this farm. But my idea is risky. If this doesn't work, the farm could go under. And yet every single one of them in here tonight looks upon me as if they don't have a doubt in the world I can pull this off.

I love my family.

♦

I FOLLOW TRIXIE, Ry, and Larkin out the front door and onto the porch. Ry is carrying a paper bag filled with leftovers. Larkin and I are empty-handed because there wasn't that much food left, and Trixie and Ry called dibs on it.

The four of us march down the steps to the cars sitting in the driveway. Laken, Mely, and Lowe stayed behind, content to sit around the kitchen table and drink coffee while they eat a second slice of pie. I'm going to put in a shift at Chesty's, Larkin has to get some baking done at her shop, and Ry said he has an important motion to argue tomorrow morning that he has to prepare for.

Trixie and Ry wave goodbye with promises that we need to get together soon. Larkin and I walk toward our vehicles, which are parked beside each other.

"I'm really impressed with your vineyard idea, Colt," she says as she reaches her driver-side door.

"Thanks, sis," I tell her with a little emotion catching in my voice. "That means a lot."

"Will you let me know what I can do to help? Even if you need an influx of money, I've got some saved up."

I hold up my hand and shake my head. "No way. I'm good on money, but I appreciate the offer."

She gives me an older sister indulgent smile. Her offer to

help will never go away, and I'll probably never accept.

I start to turn toward my car, but then remember something else I was curious about, and she is just the person to ask. "I was in Crump's grocery this morning, and I overheard Andy in there talking to Billy. He was talking about Darby, and it sounded like he was sweet on her. You might not have to worry about Andy mooning over you anymore."

Larkin rolls her eyes. The truth is she was never worried about Andy Forrester mooning over her. It was an absolute unrequited crush on his part, and he knew she was never going to look his way like that.

And I really wasn't bringing this up to Larkin to tease her, but more to feel out some stuff about Darby. Because when I was in Crump's this morning and heard Andy tell Billy he was thinking about asking Darby out for dinner, my hackles rose. I have no clue why or from where the proprietary feelings came, but I did not like the idea of Andy being sweet on Darby. He's a nice guy and has potential for a single woman.

Not that Darby is single, but she will be soon.

"So is Darby sweet on Andy?" I ask, trying to sound nonchalant and only mildly curious.

Larkin gives a shrug. "How would I know? She was in the backseat of his patrol car for all of five minutes when he drove us home Saturday night. We dropped her off first and even though both of us were pretty buzzed, I don't think we even actually talked to Andy."

"What did you talk about?" This is crucial information because there's something about Darby that intrigues Andy. A man doesn't just decide to ask someone out on a date because they have a pretty face.

Or at least I don't. There has to be substance for sure.

"We were kind of doing girly talk," Larkin says evasively.

"Girly talk?"

"Yeah. Girly talk. You know… The type of talk you only talk about with your girlfriend."

"Clearly, I don't know what that is as I don't have a girl-friend nor am I a girl," I point out.

Larkin gives a snorting type of laugh. "I believe we were talking about Darby's marriage and why it ended."

Now that's weird. What could possibly have Andy in-trigued about Darby if they were only discussing a failed marriage? Unless he was seeing an opportunity to take advantage of Darby.

I give a shake of my head. Andy's not like that. He's a genuinely good guy. If I had to take a guess, he probably listened to Darby and Larkin doing their girly talk and it came through loud and clear that Darby is a good woman. In the handful of conversations I've had with her, I've come to that conclusion as well. It probably took me all of five minutes to realize it, too.

I sidle up closer to my sister and rest my hand on the roof of her car. "So what is the deal with Darby's marriage?"

Now, we have probably entered the territory that could either be considered local gossip or it could be said I'm delving into a secret confidence Darby entrusted Larkin with. When Larkin leans back in toward me with sparkling eyes, I know Darby isn't expecting secrecy from anything she told Larkin.

"Well, it seems her soon-to-be ex-husband is a bit of a control freak and a manipulator. She got married young and got pregnant with Linnie while she was trying to work on her PhD. Her husband sort of strong-armed her into being a stay-at-home mom with promises she could go back and complete her degree later. The only problem was every time she wanted to do it, he would find a way to manipulate her into staying home. I think it was just a generally unhappy type of marriage and she wasn't fulfilled."

Well that doesn't sound scandalous at all. It sounds pretty realistic as to how I bet many marriages die. People just want different things.

Larkin leans even closer in, though. "I did kind of get from her that her husband's really a jerk. It appears he had been having an affair, although I'm not quite sure that's exactly what caused the marriage to end. Darby doesn't speak ill of him, but I can just tell by her demeanor she's had a rough time of it with him."

Once again, my hackles rise at the thought of anyone hurting Darby, and that is most definitely a strange sensation when I hardly even know her.

"Why are you so curious?" Larkin asks with wide innocent eyes. Surely she can't think my interest is just in being neighborly, can she?

She just stares at me, unsuspecting of anything.

So I go with it.

"No particular reason," I tell—well, lie—to her. "Just curious."

CHAPTER 9

Darby

I'VE BEEN LIVING in Whynot, North Carolina for just over two weeks now, and it's high time I've had breakfast again at Central Café. This isn't my first time here as I visited once before with Jake and Laken. But it is my first time as a resident of Whynot, and I've been told that all the best gossip is filtered through here.

I thought it was hilarious when two nights ago, Colt told me Central Café was the place where he heard I removed my grant application from consideration. I thought he may have been pulling my leg, but that night Larkin assured me the gossip mill in Whynot is a fully functioning news source.

To take best advantage of any potential gossip I might eavesdrop in on, I choose to sit at the diner counter that runs the length of the restaurant. It's got a white Formica top with gold speckles and aluminum swivel stools with red vinyl seats. I also make the choice to sit at the counter because I notice Floyd sitting there, the owner of the hardware store who protects the town by night with his shotgun. While I don't know this for sure, my gut instinct is he's a major source of gossip.

Now, I am not a gossiper by nature. But I find it fascinating this is such an everyday part of life in this area, and I kind of want to experience it. Larkin told me how when her brother Lowe was in a battle with his wife over their current house that she had bought from the family, she knew all about their courtship and dating not from her brother but from the gossip mill.

When I sit down right beside Floyd, he turns to look at me. I get a polite nod but before he can turn away, I stick my right hand over to him. "Hi. I'm Darby McCulhane. The new operations manager at Farrington Farms."

He grunts and then grumbles, "Pleasure to meet you. Saw you and your daughter coming out of Sweet Cakes the other day."

He takes my hand in his big meaty paw and gives it a vigorous shake.

"Want some coffee, honey?" a woman says from behind the counter. She looks to be in about her fifties, and she wears a classic waitress uniform in buttery-yellow polyester with a white Peter Pan collar. She has iron-gray hair parted down the middle and secured at the back of her neck in a tight bun covered by a hairnet. Her name tag says Muriel.

"I'd love some coffee. And a breakfast menu."

She doesn't move to get the coffee, but rather leans her hip on the counter in front of me and says, "You're Jake's kin, aren't you?"

I smile at her in return. "His sister-in-law. Well, sort of. He used to be married to my sister Kelly. But they remained great friends and so Jake is still a great friend to me. In fact, I still consider him to be a brother."

"That's sweet. He seems like a nice fella, and sure does put a twinkle in Laken's eye," she says with a swoony sigh. Then she leans in closer to me, lowering her voice to a whisper. "But I sense trouble in paradise. I think it's going to be mighty hard for those two with long distance separating them."

I try to moderate my grin, elation coursing through me. I have now been officially inducted into the Whynot gossip mill. When I lean in closer to her, I note Floyd even leans toward us so he can listen. "I think they're going to be just fine."

Muriel just blinks at me, seemingly waiting for me to say something juicier than what I just did. I glance at Floyd to find him staring at me as well, and there's no mistaking the expectancy in his eyes.

I shrug and give them an apologetic look. "Sorry. I'm just not privy to any deeper information at this point."

"But you'd share with us if you were, right?" This from Floyd in his deep baritone voice.

"Absolutely," I say with confidence, although I'm not quite sure I would. I guess it depends on the subject matter. For example, if I had inside information Jake was going to do something epically romantic, I'd spill the beans to my new friends. But if I felt that their relationship could be going south, I'd keep that close to the vest.

"You know Andy Forrester is sweet on you," Muriel says, and it takes me a moment to realize we've switched gossip gears.

"Oh, well," I start to stammer. "I'm not... well, you see... now isn't a good time to—"

"You're not in the market," Muriel concludes.

"Not really," I mutter but for some strange reason, I think about Colt Mancinkus and my denial seems a little out of place.

"Andy's a good guy, but you're still trying to get over that total jerk of a husband," Muriel continues.

I rear backward over her proclamation, almost flinging myself off the barstool. "Excuse me?"

Muriel nods knowingly, her eyes swimming in sympathy. "You know… because he was all controlling and didn't let you pursue your dreams. Held you back so your life was unfulfilled."

How in the hell would she know anything about Mitch? I mean, her information is accurate, but I'm totally thrown for a loop.

"Andy was in here a bit ago," Floyd says by way of explanation.

Then a light bulb goes off in my head. Andy had given Larkin and me a ride home Saturday night, which I thought was an odd thing for a police officer on duty to do, but whatever. I was close to drunk. So was Larkin. And we talked.

A lot.

I shake my head with a smile, not able to be mad at anyone for poking in my business when I was so loudly proclaiming it. I look to Muriel and then to Floyd. "It's a complicated situation, but one I'm finally free of. I'm just happy to be starting a new life here in Whynot."

My words must be definitive enough they don't invite more questions. Muriel turns away. Grabbing a white ceramic mug from a stack, she also snags a coffee pot from a burner on the back counter. As she pours for me, I flip through a menu Floyd slid over my way.

"I'll take two eggs over easy, some hash browns, and a side of bacon."

Muriel is shaking her head and clucking her tongue. "You got to have biscuits and gravy."

"But I don't want biscuits and gravy."

"Yes, you do," Floyd says from beside me. "Trust me on this."

I turn back to Muriel and incline my head. "Fine. I'll take

a side of biscuits and gravy. But I want my eggs, hash browns, and bacon as well."

Muriel winks at me. "I like a girl with a hearty appetite."

"Me too," a deep voice says from my other side, and I turn to find Colt sliding onto the stool to my right. An electric zing of awareness ripples through me and by my reaction to his presence, it's clear that perhaps I have some interest where he's concerned.

It's a warm day for early October, and the forecast said it was going to get into the mid-eighties. Colt is wearing a pair of cargo shorts and a faded navy-blue T-shirt with running shoes. I'm going to guess he's not working on the farm today.

"Good morning," I say with a smile.

Muriel clearly doesn't need to ask Colt what he wants. She merely slides a cup of black coffee in front of him and says, "Your order will be up in a jiff, sugar."

"Thanks, Muriel." Colt then leans forward to look past me to greet Floyd. "What's up with you, Floyd? I haven't seen you around lately."

Floyd turns to Colt and I lean back in my stool, so they have a clear line of sight to each other. I notice he's got a tiny piece of egg stuck in his beard. "Been trying to chase off those damn coyotes that are coming into town. They seem to be hanging out behind Mainer House. I don't want to kill them, but just hoping to scare 'em off with a few shotgun blasts. Mely yelled at me the other night that I'm scaring her half to death, though. Maybe I can set traps for them."

I find it incredibly sweet and endearing this big bear of a man who prowls around town with a shotgun has too tender of a heart to shoot coyotes. Just another example of the complex layers I'm finding to the people around here.

"So how bad was your hangover on Sunday?" Colt asks

me, and I turn away from Floyd to look at the impossibly handsome man sitting beside me.

I give a shake of my head. "Not hung over at all."

Colt's eyebrows shoot up. "That's impressive. You and Larkin put away quite a few beers Saturday night."

"It was over a long period of time. And I drank plenty of water before I went to bed," I admit.

He nods at me sagely, knowing that staying hydrated is the best way to defeat a hangover.

Floyd pushes off his stool and mutters, "I'm out of here. You folks have a nice day."

Colt and I give farewells, and Muriel blows him a kiss from behind the counter. She then turns around to the counter behind which a cook is frying up all kinds of delicious-smelling things and grabs two plates he had just put up there. Muriel places our breakfast orders in front of us and I have to admit, the side of biscuits and gravy looks really good.

I start to cut into it for a bite, and Colt shakes his head. "You got a doctor that up first, Darby."

"Doctor it up?"

He grabs a bottle of Texas Pete hot sauce from a condiment tray before him and slides it to me. He doesn't say a word, but just nods to the bottle.

I shrug and take it, twisting the cap that is crusted with dried hot sauce off. After I put a few liberal dashes of red peppery liquid over the gravy, I dig in.

Colt and I both eat in silence for a few moments and I try hard not to moan in delight from how good the food tastes. There is nothing quite like finding a really good diner for some scratch country cooking.

Colt sets his utensils down and takes a sip of his coffee.

When he sets his mug back on the counter, he turns slightly on his stool to face me. "So how are things going over at Farrington Farms? I heard a rumor you've got Carlos making some cheese."

I chuckle and wipe my mouth with my napkin. "Yeah, with the farm leasing out most of the land, there's just not an awful lot to keep Carlos busy full time. He suggested using the goats milk to make cheese the way the original owner did. I thought it was a good idea, so he's been spending a lot of time in the kitchen."

"Carlos is a good man," Colt tells me. "He did some work on our farm before he had to go back to Texas because of a sick family member. You can't go wrong with him whether it's in the kitchen or working the farm."

I nod and pick my fork back up again. "What about you? When are you going to actually start building up your vineyard?"

"Already started actually," Colt says, and I can hear the excitement in his voice. It makes me glad he got the grant. "We're spending the rest of this week building the trellises and will be planting the vines next week. I hired on some extra crew with part of the grant money."

"How many acres?" I ask.

"Well, I can expect anywhere from two to ten tons of yield per acre once the vines start producing. I can get two barrels of wine out of a ton of grapes. It would be a minimum of fourteen hundred bottles of wine per acre if the yield is low and over five thousand if it's high. I'm thinking I'll start with ten acres."

I whistle low and look at him with round eyes. "That's quite an endeavor."

Colt gives me a nod, and I can see some anxiety in his

eyes. "I'm leveraging everything on this. The entire grant as well as removing some of the land we had previously leased. So the income into the farm is going to drop. But I figure go big or go home."

"Do you have any plans to supplement the income somehow?"

Colt gives me a confident smile. "I've been wanting to do this winery for several years now and to prepare for it, I have been increasing our cattle operation. It's going to be a little bit tight for the next couple of years, but it's manageable."

"It sounds like you've really got all of your ducks in a row, Colt. I have a feeling this is going to be an enormous success for you."

His eyes pin me in place and his voice gets a little low. "Seriously, Darby. I want to thank you again for stepping back from the grant. I couldn't have done this without it. You may not realize this, but your actions have probably saved my family."

A large lump of emotion sticks solidly in my throat, and I take a sip of coffee to try to dislodge it. I blink my eyes hard so I don't cry, and offer Colt something else. "Would you like any of my help or advice on the nutrient side of things? I'm kind of brainy and geeky when it comes to that stuff."

Colt gives a booming laugh and picks up his coffee cup. He looks at me across the edge after he takes a sip and says, "I would love for any help or advice you can give me. In fact, if you have time this week, I'd love for you to come out and look at things."

My lips involuntarily peel back into a big smile, completely charmed by Colt's enthusiasm and gratitude and let's face it, his gorgeous good looks. "How about tomorrow?"

"It's a date," Colt says.

CHAPTER 10

Colt

I CHECK THE tension indicator spring, noting it's a few pounds short. This prompts me to give a few cranks on the tension strainer, and I check the spring again.

Perfect. Rigged to withhold two hundred and fifty pounds of grapes.

I wipe the back of my arm across my forehead, removing the layer of sweat that has formed. Even though it's in the upper sixties today, the nature of the work we are doing building the grape trellises is strenuous.

And these aren't the flimsy type of lattice trellises that most people think of. These are large T-shaped timbers sunk into the ground twenty feet apart with tension wire strung between that will support the heavy vines. They aren't pretty, but they are functional.

"Boss... got a visitor," one of the workers operating the auger two rows over calls out to me.

I hold my hand up over my eyes to shield them from the sunshine and see an aqua-blue Ford F250 long bed truck—a mid-sixties' model—bouncing down the dirt road toward us. The smile that comes unbidden to my face when Darby hops out of the truck is proof positive I enjoy her company.

I grab my T-shirt I had discarded from one of the overhead wires and put it on. Just as I'm yanking it down over my stomach, Darby is close enough she can tease me in a low voice, "No need to put your shirt on in front of me."

Her face is beaming with amusement, and she looks extraordinarily bubbly today. She's wearing her blonde hair up in a high ponytail, and she's rocking a pair of jeans, a long-sleeved thermal T-shirt, and work boots. Not quite sure when that type of clothing for women became attractive to me, but I find I like it very much.

"Gotta get dressed," I tease her back. "Don't want to discombobulate that brain of yours with all my male glory."

Darby's laugh is melodic and bubbly all at the same time. Her gaze turns to the trellis I've been working on, and she gives a nod toward it. "These look fantastic."

"I decided to go with a double-curtain trellis," I tell her as I study the several acres we've already built up.

"Smart," she praises as she takes in her surroundings. "More sunlight through the top of the vines equals a greater yield."

"Exactly," I agree.

We set the pressure-treated trellises so the rows are ten feet apart, which will eventually allow me to bring in harvesting machinery down the road. Until then, I'm going to be doing a lot of grape picking with some seasonal help to save on costs.

"Nice truck." I nod at the vehicle she had pulled up in.

Darby chuckles as she peers over her shoulder at it. "It's Carlos's truck. He told me I shouldn't be driving my Beemer on the farm roads."

"He'd be right about that."

"I'm going to trade my car in for a truck once I can find some time. Definitely a newer model than Carlos's because I would never be able to survive without air conditioning in the summer."

Summer is a good seven months away. That means Darby is here for the long haul.

My stomach rumbles, and I look down at my watch. Almost noon. I take Darby's elbow and turn her toward my Gator. "Let's go get some lunch."

"Lunch?" she asks in surprise but walks peaceably by my side.

As we climb into the Gator, I explain, "Up at the main house. Mama always fixes a good lunch."

"I don't want to impose," Darby says.

We take off with a lurching jump forward, which causes Darby to grab hold of the roll bar. I chuckle and explain to her how things work in the South. "My mama would have my hide if she knew you were here at a mealtime and I didn't bring you to the house to eat. That's just the way we do things around here."

Darby beams a bright smile. "Then by all means, I would like to preserve your hide. Let's go have lunch."

I take Darby the long way back to the house, so she can see more of the farm. I point out the sections we have currently leased but explain the crops we used to grow on them. She has lots of questions about the way we grow and harvest. I take her past pastures that hold the cattle and finally past Mainer Lake.

I point across the southern end of the lake. "That's where I live. It used to be my brother Lowe's but since he moved into Mainer House, I hated to see that little cabin sitting empty."

"It's beautiful," Darby exclaims.

Nodding, I tell her, "I love looking out over the lake in the morning at sunrise. Lowe built it all by himself."

Darby gives a low whistle. "That's impressive."

"All of my siblings are impressive," I say with a burst of pride. "Every one of them is so very accomplished."

Darby turns to regard me thoughtfully while she holds tightly to the bar. We bump along the dirt road filled with more potholes than not, but it doesn't prevent conversation. "You're close to your siblings, aren't you?"

I give her a nonchalant shrug. "We fight more than not. But yeah, pretty close. We get together every Sunday for dinner at Mama's. Even though that's about the only time we get to see each other during the week because we're all so busy, it's like no time has passed in between. Know what I mean?"

Darby nods vigorously, and her face softens. "That's how it is with my sister Kelly. She's almost nine years older than me and often acted like a mother figure growing up, but we're extremely close. We don't get to see each other often, but we talk all the time by phone."

We skirt past the lake and through a small trail that traverses through a thick copse of pine trees, continuing by the big gray barn that we open to the town of Whynot for the Lantern Festival every summer, and through another copse of trees before the farmhouse comes into view. Darby breathes out, "Oh, that house is so pretty."

I think we have one of the prettiest houses in Scuppernong County. It's massive… Three stories and covered in gray clapboard siding with white trim. Mama had the shutters painted burgundy about a decade ago, and I note they could use a little touch up. As with most farmhouses, there's a wide porch across the front she has studded with burgundy-colored rocking chairs and tiny tables with plants on them. The right side of the house has a detached double garage Lowe and I helped Dad build several years ago. There's about an acre of lawn surrounding the house with nothing but fields all around. Just a few months ago, it was green with field corn that's all harvested now.

I lead Darby into the house. She peeks into the formal living room, which is decorated well… formally. Delicate cherry furniture with a flowered print that makes me nauseated to look at. I always feel like the furniture is going to crumble under me if I sit on it. I much prefer the den at the back of the house that's filled with heavy leather furniture and cushy recliners.

"Is that you Colt?" my mama calls from the back of the house.

"It's me," I holler as I start walking that way. "And I've got company."

My mama says, "Excellent," as we enter the kitchen, where she's pulling out a loaf of fresh bread from the oven.

After she sets it on the stovetop, she wipes her hands on her apron and turns to face us. She gives me a sweet smile, but her eyes only stay on me for a moment.

They light on my lunch companion, and her smile grows wider. "You must be Darby, the new peach farmer come to town."

Darby smiles and steps forward with her hand stretched out to shake my mom's. My mama isn't having any of that and manages to wrap Darby up into a long, hard hug of welcome. Darby has absolutely no hesitation in giving my mom a good squeeze back, which tells me that she is generally an affectionate type of person. Don't know why this pleases me so much.

When my mom pulls back, she points to the table and orders us both, "Go. Sit. I'll grab you some ice tea."

"What's for lunch?" I ask, my belly rumbling again.

"I'm just going to throw together some club sandwiches with the fresh bread I just made, and I made a fruit salad," she says as she walks to the refrigerator to pull out a pitcher of sweet tea. She fills two glasses and brings them over to us.

I watch as Darby takes a sip and then wrinkles her nose as she pulls it away from her mouth. I laugh and say, "Haven't gotten used to the sweet tea yet, have you?"

She gives a quick shake of her head. "I actually like it. It just takes me by surprise the first time I drink it."

"I can get you something else," Mama says solicitously.

Darby waves her away. "I really do like it. Is there anything I can do to help you?"

Before my mom can answer, I tell Darby how things are done in the South. "You are a guest in our home and as such, you are prohibited from helping. In fact, southern etiquette dictates you have to sit there, drink your sweet tea, and engage in idle gossip with us."

All three of us laugh, and Mama goes back to the refrigerator to pull out the makings of our sandwiches.

While she's slicing into the fresh bread, I further educate Darby. "But the next time you come to our house, you are considered family and you are more than welcome to help all you like."

"Duly noted," Darby says with a laugh.

"So how are you and your daughter settling in?" my mother asks as she builds up our sandwiches from the center kitchen island.

Darby gives a sigh through her nose before answering. "I'm settling in great. It's wonderful to be working on the orchard, and I've always loved farm life. But it's been a bit of an adjustment for Linnie."

"How old is she?" Mom asks.

"Seven."

"Oh, that's such a great age. How about you and Linnie come join us for Sunday supper at two this coming weekend? I'd love to meet her, and we'll show her how great this town is."

"That's just so nice," Darby says in a soft voice full of gratitude. She will try anything to help Linnie along. "I'll accept for both of us. She's missing a lot of things from back home, so this will be good for her."

"I can imagine," Mama commiserates. And because she has no boundaries, which is born only from a natural empathy for other people, she says, "Divorce is never easy on anyone. I imagine Linnie must be very confused."

I can't help but cringe internally because that was an overly forward statement. But to my surprise, and probably because my mother just has a way of bringing those things out in people, Darby has no qualms with talking about it. "The split from Darby's father, Mitch, was pretty contentious. He didn't want us to leave, and Linnie sort of fed into that."

"Are she and her father really close?" Mama asks.

I sit back further in my chair, just listening to these two women talk. I'm obviously fascinated by Darby, and I am a grateful beneficiary of the information my mother is pulling out of her.

Darby shrugs and taps her fingers on her glass. "No, they're not close. Mitch is sort of a hands-off father."

Now what the heck does that mean?

Leave it up to Mama to get that question answered for me. "Let me guess, he's one of those men with old-fashioned ideas that the womenfolk raise the children and the menfolk retire to the study with their cigars and brandy after dinner, while the women clean up."

I stare at my mom in disbelief, my eyes about ready to pop out of my head. I wouldn't necessarily categorize Catherine Mainer as a feminist, but she is definitely a modern woman and believes a couple should share equally in all burdens. Still, there is no mistaking the condescension in her voice.

Darby gives a light laugh and nods at my mama, who is stacking the sandwiches on a platter. "You pretty much just described Mitch McCulhane. So to answer your original question, Linnie just doesn't have much of a bond with him. I mean, there's love there, because he's her dad. But her reservations and anger about moving here aren't so much about leaving him as they are all the things that gave her comfort back home. It's the only home she's ever known, and I just think she needs to adjust."

My mom and Darby continue to chat, moving on to things not of such a personal nature. I sort of tune them out, contemplating what I've learned about Darby so far. Between what Larkin told me and what Darby said today, it sounds like her husband is quite the jerk. I'm having a tough time comprehending, though, how Darby put up with that for so long. Every bit I have come to know about her tells me she is a strong and independent woman, and I can't imagine her being pushed and confined into a certain role.

Not that the role of being a mother is bad, but clearly Darby is the type of woman who wants to work and can accomplish so much in her life. I'm sure there was some valid reason why she let her soon-to-be ex-husband keep her from pursuing those dreams, but I'm not going to get those answers today.

I'll wait until she's ready to talk about those things on her own.

CHAPTER 11

Colt

I GIVE A quick honk of my truck's horn as I pull up in front of the Farrington barn. I texted Darby about half an hour ago and asked her if I could stop by. She responded quickly with a, "Sure. I'll be in the barn."

The rolling doors are both open, and I can see Darby stacking bags in the corner. Hopping out of my truck, I grab the two containers Mama loaded me up with before I walked out the door to come over here.

Darby meets me just outside the barn, dusting her hands off on her jeans, which are smudged with dirt and grass stains on her knees.

"What have you got there?" she asks as she eyes the plastic Tupperware.

"A thank-you gift," I tell her as I hand over containers. "Mama made some pound cake and cut up some strawberries for you to have shortcake."

"Why is your mama thanking me?" she says with a laugh. She takes the containers and holds them up to look through the opaque side.

"Well, actually I'm the one who's thanking you for the help you gave me the other day after lunch. I didn't realize I was so deficient in soil nutrient knowledge. I conned Mama into making that for you, but it's my way of saying thank you."

"I love strawberry shortcake," Darby says with appreciation. "But this was totally not necessary. I was glad to help."

Her eyes are bright and sparkling in the mid-afternoon sun. I wish she was more of a chore to look at because I could pretty much stand here for a long time and just stare at her. She's prettier than any girl I've ever known.

After a moment, I realize both of us are just looking at each other and an awkward silence ensues. My true intent in coming over here was only to thank her for her time and knowledge she provided me for the vineyard. She's more knowledgeable on crop sciences than anyone I've ever met before. But I can't lie and say I wasn't excited to actually see Darby.

Talk to her.

Spend a little bit of time with her.

I'm in this weird place where I have definite interest in her, but I really don't know how or if I should even pursue it. She's just come out of a bad marriage and is new to town. She's trying to set up a peach orchard, which has got to be stressful in addition to the hours of hard work I know she's putting in. She also has a daughter who is not quite happy to be here, and all of that adds up to a woman who probably couldn't give a turtle's butt about some hick farmer interested in her.

And just like that, I talk myself out of Darby McCulhane.

This is a bad idea.

With a nod of my head, I give her a smile. "Well, I better get out of your hair. I'm sure you've got stuff to do and so do I."

"Thanks again for the shortcake," she says softly, and is that regret I'm not staying I hear in her voice?

No. Don't think like that.

Turning to my truck, I toss my hand up in acknowledgment and call back, "See you later."

Three paces is about all I take before Darby calls out, "Wait a minute... Colt... are you interested in seeing where I'm going to be placing the orchard?"

I spin around way too fast, and I'm sure the eager look at my face conveys just how lame I am. "If you have time, I'd love to see it."

Swearing to God I will not make anything of the fact Darby looks both relieved and excited that I've agreed to stay, I follow her into the barn where she sets the shortcake and strawberries on a wooden counter built into the wall. We then load up on her Gator, which looks very similar to mine, and she drives us out of the barn. She hangs a left, and we head out directly over a soybean field that was harvested not all that long ago.

Farrington Farms isn't quite as large as Mainer Farms, and most of their land is leased just like ours. The prior owner, Bob Farrington, unexpectedly sold this place, and Darby's former brother-in-law, Jake McDaniel, had bought it. He bought it for a tax write-off and to give Darby a second chance in life but knowing Jake, I think the tax write-off isn't really what he cares about.

We ride past the goat pasture, and I see MG kicking and bouncing around just inside the enclosure. MG is short for Ms. Goatikins, and she's a baby goat that became unnaturally bonded to Jake after she was born. She's only recently started taking a bottle from Carlos and drinking from her dam.

"I took some soil samples today to check the pH and nutrient levels. The pH was a little low."

"That explains the bags of dolomite I saw you stacking in the barn. You should let me move all that for you."

Darby looks at me briefly with a smile. "You're sweet. But I got it. I'm going to put them out tomorrow."

"By yourself?" I ask.

"Well, Carlos will help me."

"You're going to spread dolomite on thirty acres?" I ask incredulously.

Darby gives a husky laugh that sort of punches me in the gut and shakes her head. "I'm actually going to use a tractor to apply it. I was able to rent one from a guy Floyd turned me on to."

"Bart Stephenson," I say confidently. He's got a ton of equipment he's collected over his years of farming, and will often rent out tractors, backhoes, augers, and the like.

"That's right. He gave me a good deal, too."

We spend about half an hour driving over the portion of land Darby has sectioned off for the orchard. One of the great things about central North Carolina is it has an endless supply of rolling hills. She chose to set the orchard on an eastern-facing slope that would provide excellent drainage and sun exposure.

She tells me in addition to trying different applications of nutrients to alter yield and quality, she's also going to space the trees out at varying lengths to see if the higher density would affect the yield. She speaks for quite a while but loses me about halfway through.

I guess she notices the blank look on my face because she gives me a light punch on my shoulder and exclaims, "I'll have to pull out some graphs and charts and show you that way."

I give an exaggerated yawn. "Boring."

Her laughter is as bright and sunny as the day and is way more uplifting than any laugh should be.

Just as we are pulling the gator back into the barn, I see

one of the county school buses stop out on the highway at the end of the gravel driveway. Linnie gets off the bus, and then waves to another little girl who's hanging out one of the open windows. She's smiling as she turns to trudge down the lane, hitching her backpack up higher on her shoulders.

Darby comes up to stand beside me as we watch her daughter walking our way. Her voice sounds somewhat relieved and hopeful when she murmurs, "She's smiling. That's a good sign. She must've had a good day today."

"Doesn't she like school?" I ask.

"She did back in Illinois. She's very smart and was at the top of her class. I think she's just trying to make friends and get her footing here, though."

Sadly, I can't relate to that. I've lived in Whynot my entire life. Even more constraining is the fact I've lived on Mainer Farms my entire life. I'm not sure if I could be any more lame if I tried.

Linnie looks up from her intense study of the gravel she walks upon, taking note of her mom and me standing just outside the barn. Her expression becomes guarded as she slows her walk.

"How was school today, honey?" Darby asks. Linnie comes to a dead stop about twenty feet from us.

Her gaze slides from her mother to me, and her eyes narrow just a little. I feel like a spotlight is on me, but I hold my stare on her until she's forced to look back at her mom.

"It sucked," she mutters and turns toward the house.

We watch in silence as Linnie trudges up the porch steps and disappears into the house.

Darby gives a deep sigh and winces with apology. "Sorry about that."

"What do you have to be sorry about?" I ask her with my

head tilted slightly. "She's a kid. I've totally heard worse."

Darby shakes her head in what I take to be frustration and puts her hands on her hips. She lets her gaze trail back to the house. "I've got to figure something out. We haven't had much time together since we've moved down here. She started school right away, and I've been busy getting things set up at the farm."

"Which is exactly why both of you need to come hang out with the Mancinkus clan on Sunday for dinner."

Darby's eyes crinkle and light up. "I'm really looking forward to it."

"Does Linnie like to sing?" I ask.

She gives me back a confused look. "Sing?"

I nod. "I might just have to pull out my guitar and teach her some good old knee-slapping, foot-stomping country songs."

"You play the guitar?" she asks, eyes twinkling even brighter.

"I've got layers you couldn't even begin to imagine." I start walking backward toward my truck, so I don't have to take my eyes off Darby. I point my finger at her and say, "Two o'clock on Sunday. Both of you prepare to be entertained and well fed."

Darby's delighted chuckle follows me into my truck until I close the door.

I look through my rearview mirror as I drive down the lane of Farrington Farms. Darby doesn't move from her spot, but watches me the entire way until I disappear.

CHAPTER 12

Colt

I'M BACK AT Farrington Farms. It's a different day, slightly different story.

I pull my truck up right in front of Darby's house. I hadn't expected to be back here this Sunday morning, but after I hung up the phone with Darby not too long ago, I decided to take matters into my own hands. This morning when Darby called to regretfully inform me that she and Linnie could not attend Sunday dinner with my family, it hit me like a wrecking ball that my interest in Darby extends far beyond just mere intrigue into this fascinating woman. I now fully admit I've come to like her.

Strange.

I've never used the word "hate" in my life to describe my feelings for someone, but before I ever met Darby, I intensely disliked her. It's not lost on me that within just a matter of moments of meeting and talking to her, my entire perception changed. Darby really let herself get into trouble with me when she made the bold move to pull her application for the expansion grant from consideration. Yes, Darby is one of the most beautiful women I have ever known, but she became infinitely more attractive when I realized she has a heart of gold.

So here I am at her house, unbidden and possibly unwelcome, to make it known I have an interest in her. And if I'm interested in her, it means I have to be interested in Linnie.

After I hung up the phone with Darby, I had a new person I intensely disliked.

Her husband, Mitch.

"I'm really sorry, Colt," Darby had explained on the phone not but half an hour ago. "But we're not going to be able to come to supper today."

"Why?" I asked quite simply.

She had no hesitation in admitting, "It's Linnie. She's just… in a mood, I guess. She's flat-out refusing to go. While I could certainly force her and drag her to your house, it would not be a pleasant experience for any of your family."

"What's the reason for the mood?" I could sense by the tone of her voice that something had happened to put Linnie in her funk.

Darby didn't answer right away. I could read into her pause she was trying to figure out whether she should share a burden with me. So I urged her. "Talk to me, Darby. What's going on?"

There was no hesitation after that. She let it all come out in a rushing confession of frustration. "Her father called her this morning. I could only hear her end of the conversation, but it was clear he was in full-out attack mode on me. I could tell that whatever he was saying on his end, he was trying to manipulate Linnie into putting pressure on me to come back to Illinois."

I didn't push her for the details. I can imagine some of the things a parent might say to an impressionable seven-year-old to turn them against the other parent. While I don't have any firsthand experience with such things, I've had plenty of friends and acquaintances over the years who have gone through bitter divorces and custody struggles. I'm aware there are some people in the world who will use their kid as a weapon.

Yeah, I don't like this Mitch dude.

I assured Darby there would be other Sunday dinners they could come to. I put her mind at ease by saying I completely understood what she was going through, even though I don't. The only thing I did understand is I had made a new friend in Darby McCulhane. I thought she was a good woman. She's struggling right now to get situated into a new home and is very far away from everything that provided her security.

She helped me out and by extension helped my family out when she gave up the expansion grant.

I'm going to return the favor.

I turn my truck off and hop out with determination. After jogging up the creaky porch steps, I give three solid raps with my knuckles on the wood casing of the screen door. Within moments, Darby's opening it and blinking at me in surprise.

"Good morning," I say cheerily.

Darby pushes open the screen door wider and steps back in silent invitation. As I brush past her, she asks, "What are you doing here?"

"I've come to kidnap your daughter," I tell her.

I did not expect this to alarm Darby, so it was not surprising to see the corners of her mouth tip upward. "Kidnap my daughter? I just want to make sure I heard that correctly."

I grin and nod. "Cross my heart I won't corrupt her or anything."

Darby stares at me for a few moments and while she's clearly amused, I can see a little bit of distance in her eyes—not because she doesn't trust me, but because she doesn't want to place her burdens on my doorstep.

I give her a reassuring smile. "I'm going to take her horseback riding. You told me the other day when you came over to have lunch that she had a horse and it was one of the things she really missed."

It's not hard to figure out that the rapid blinking of Darby's eyes means she's trying to dispel some wet emotion my offer has caused. The last thing I want to do is make a lady cry, so I also add on with a wink, "And that way, you can have a few hours of relaxation all to yourself. Maybe go get your nails done or your hair fixed up all pretty or something. Not that it isn't pretty as is, but you know... spend some time on Darby."

She just stares at me in disbelief. That lasts for only about three seconds before she snaps her head to the right and yells up the stairs, "Linnie. Get down here."

The footsteps overhead are far too heavy to belong to a seven-year-old. The way she's stomping through the house above us indicates she is not a happy kid. She comes down the staircase with her shoulders hunched forward. When she reaches the bottom landing, she glares at her mom and says, "What?"

It's not quite belligerent, but it is rude.

As I was raised by a Marine Corps drill instructor father with no patience for smart talk and a strong, southern woman who insists on manners, a crappy attitude has never been something tolerated in our family. I want to tell Linnie to have some respect for her mother, but that would put us off on the wrong foot.

To my surprise, Darby makes it known she doesn't find her daughter's attitude acceptable. She narrows her eyes slightly, and says in an even but firm voice, "Remember what we said? You need to check your attitude at your bedroom door. I don't care if you want to stay up there and sulk but when you're in my presence, I expect you to be pleasant."

Linnie doesn't respond, but her cheeks turn pink.

Darby glances to me and inclines her head my way before telling Linnie, "Colt is here to take you horseback riding if you would like to go."

There's no doubt in my mind I made the right decision in coming here when Linnie's entire face lights up with joy. Her head snaps my way so fast her glasses slide down to the end of her nose. She just pushes them right back up as she asks, "Really?"

I nod. "I've got a good buddy who has a few horses, and he's got two ready for you and me to saddle up for some trail riding."

It's also made clear to me that despite Linnie's sullen attitude toward her mom, she was actually raised with good manners. She immediately turns to Darby. In a very sweet yet imploring voice, she asks, "Can I go, Mom? Please."

Darby doesn't hesitate or make her daughter suffer. She just smiles at her and gestures toward the staircase. "Go get changed into some riding gear."

Linnie doesn't need to be told twice. She goes flying up the stairs.

♦

IT'S PATENTLY OBVIOUS Linnie takes her horseback riding seriously. While I waited for her to get changed, Darby told me she'd been riding for a few years and it was almost on a daily basis.

My buddy, Travis Peregoy, gave Linnie a very docile mare who is on the smaller side. He kindly did the same for me, although mine is not on the smaller side. I've ridden a lot throughout my life, but it is not something I do routinely and usually only when Travis and I would go riding out in the woods to go camping. We grew up together with his family's horse farm only two miles down the road from us.

Travis pointed us to a trail that runs parallel to Crabtree Creek, and we walk along silently with pine trees providing enough shade to cool the unseasonably warm October day. If we were to continue following the creek south, we would ride right into town coming out behind Mainer House where Mely and Lowe live. I don't intend to go that far because my intent is to put Linnie in enough of an accepting mood I can ultimately convince her and her mom to still join the Mancinkus family for supper.

I ease into conversation with Linnie by talking about something that is a no-brainer. "Your mom says you've been riding for a couple of years and you have a horse at your dad's."

I didn't ask her questions, but tried to subtly open the conversation. She doesn't take the bait, and I don't get a response. This goes in line with the quiet I got on the ride over to Travis's farm, but I do chalk some of it up to shyness.

"My butt is going to be hurting something fierce tomorrow," I say casually as we walk side by side along the trail.

I glance over at Linnie to see her lips curve upward in a smile. For some reason, all kids find the word "butt" funny.

"I can set up some regular riding with Travis if you'd like," I tell her lightly, so it doesn't come off as bribing her for good behavior. "He owes me a favor or two."

He really doesn't owe me any favors, but I can set up some kind of rental of his horses' time. He'll give me a good deal—something an extra shift each week at Chesty's would easily cover.

"I want to learn how to jump horses," Linnie says, and I

have to contain the smile that wants to break out on my face that she's engaging in conversation.

"Oh yeah?" I ask curiously.

She nods and pushes her glasses up her nose. Her voice is smaller when she says, "My dad promised to get me lessons if we come back to Illinois."

What a jerk. Promising his daughter a gift that can only come to fruition if her mother decides to return to her husband. A gift with conditions is no gift at all, and that's completely setting Darby up for failure as a mother by not going back.

"Well, we don't need to wait for that to happen," I say confidently. Jumping isn't Travis's thing with his horses, but I'm sure I can figure something out. I guarantee his contacts in the horse community will turn up somebody I can get Linnie to for some lessons.

She stares at me with hopeful eyes. "Can you really do that?"

"Absolutely." Even if I have to buy a damn horse myself and kidnap an instructor to come teach her.

The happiness emanating off her little body as she sits up straighter in the saddle tells me now is a good time to have a real talk with her. There's no way in hell I'm going to talk directly about her dad because I don't trust my words. I don't know the guy, and I don't want to know the guy. I vow to myself I'll never talk about him in front of her because that's not cool.

But I've got no qualms with talking about Darby. "You said school sucked the other day. How come?"

Linnie shrugs. "Just some mean kids."

This gets my hackles up. I can't stand bullying. "Who?"

"This boy in my class. Caleb Rochelle."

I have to bite my tongue to keep from snorting. Caleb's parents went to high school with me. His mom is okay, a little on the meek side. But his dad is a big bully himself, so it's clear the apple didn't fall far from the tree.

"Want me to talk to his parents?" I ask.

She shakes her head vigorously. "No. I can handle it."

I push a little harder at her using the bullying as an opening. "I know you're struggling. With the move and now you're having to deal with a bully at school. I also know your mom is struggling."

Linnie gives a silent shrug but doesn't respond to my statement about her mother.

I push a little harder. "What's the deal, Linnie? Why are you so angry at your mom and making it so tough on her?"

Another shrug. Perhaps because she isn't quite sure why she's acting the way she is?

"I can see you don't like talking about this, but unfortunately I'm too curious for my own good." Linnie glances over with a wary gaze. "I'm going ask you five questions, but then I'm not going to mention it again… as long as you answer truthfully."

She continues gazing at me expectantly as our horses plod along. She's not in a sharing mood, but I've clearly interested her in the concept of limited questions and a promise to let it go after that.

"Was your mom happy when you were living back in Illinois with your dad?"

She shakes her head, dropping her gaze to where the reins rest loosely in her hands.

"Do you want your mom to be happy?"

She nods.

"Linnie," I call softly and wait for her to look at me. "You do understand that the failure of your parents' marriage has nothing to do with you, right?"

"I know," she says softly.

"They both love you," I tell her as our horses plod along. "You understand that, right?"

She nods and chews on her lower lip as if in contemplation.

I smile and lighten my voice into a teasing mode. "All right. As promised. Only five questions and this is the last one. Who do you want to live with? No joking around and just between you and me so I know the real Linnie. Who do you really want to live with?"

She doesn't hesitate at all. "My mom. I want to live with my mom."

I wink at her and grin. "I suspected as much. I can see right through you, kid."

Linnie giggles and blushes.

"Want to see if we can make these horses go a little faster?" My butt is not looking forward to how it's going to feel tomorrow.

Linnie answers me by tapping the heels of her little boots into the horse's flank, and we take off at a trot.

Ouch.

The things I'll do to make a kid smile.

CHAPTER 13

Darby

COLT OPENS THE passenger door, and I step out of the silver sedan he had showed up in to pick me up for dinner. I hold together the skirt portion of the plum-colored wrap dress I had put on and paired with tan high-heeled boots. Colt told me sheepishly he had borrowed his mother's car for tonight since we were dressing up. He didn't think it would be seemly for me to have to jump out of the truck in high heels. I appreciate the sentiment. I easily alight from the car without showing a slip of leg as I hold my skirt together.

I'm not quite sure how I went from Sunday dinner with the Mancinkus family to a dinner date with Colt. I imagine the answer lies somewhere in the fact that when Colt brought Linnie back home after practically kidnapping her, she seemed like a new child.

No. That's not quite right. Linnie seemed like herself again. I have no clue what happened when they went riding, but she came back different. I about had to pick my jaw up off the floor when she looked up at Colt, pushing her glasses up her nose, and asked, "Are we still invited for supper this afternoon?"

Colt had grinned down at her and tugged on one of her pigtails. "Of course you are, pipsqueak."

He'd then turned those gorgeous hazel eyes on me. "See you at two o'clock."

And Sunday dinner with the Mancinkus family was exactly what both Linnie and I needed together to help solidify our bond. Some would think hanging around with a bunch of strangers would not be conducive to that but on the contrary, there were so many foreign faces that Linnie naturally gravitated toward me. She looked up to me for security around this large, loud brood of people.

But my daughter learned soon enough these were good people.

Pap was constantly teasing her, and Mely did her hair into a fancy French braid Linnie couldn't stop staring at in the mirror.

Through casual talk before dinner started, I learned Jake and Laken had apparently committed to each other to make a go of their relationship. Jake told me he would make Whynot his permanent residence, and he would be living with Laken for the time being. She would be traveling back and forth to Chicago as needed but for the most part, he was going to try to work as much as he could from here.

This apparently made Laken very happy. Linnie kept giving side-eyed looks at her uncle Jake and Laken as they kept kissing on each other through dinner. I thought it was adorable, but Linnie is just seven and not all that interested in romance. She wrinkled her nose a time or two as she watched them.

In addition to pulling my daughter out of her funk, the other reason I am on a date tonight with Colt is because of what happened after dinner at his house. We moved from the dining room out onto the porch where Colt brought out his guitar. Catherine and Jerry, the matriarch and patriarch, sat together on a porch swing. Pap was right beside them in a rocking chair. Colt plopped down on the first porch step, leaning his back up against the railing post. Everyone else spread out among the other rockers, and Linnie sat down on the porch step next to Colt. I leaned against the wall right beside the front door and stared in amazement as Colt began to play.

His skills were amazing. A true musician. I could tell he's been playing for years.

And his voice?

Oh, wow.

Forget being a farmer. He could be a country music star with that deep rich voice as he played some Tim McGraw. He wasn't playing just for me but for the family as a whole, and yet I felt his music in a very personal way. I looked around at the family, everyone watching Colt with pride. Larkin had a dreamy look on her face as she swayed to the music. Laken was leaning her head on Jake's shoulder, and Lowe and Mely had their arms wrapped around each other. Everyone was watching Colt, and some were humming along.

Except for Pap. He was staring straight at me, and I think the old man was looking to see how I was reacting to his grandson. He had a sly smile and a twinkle in his eye, and there's no doubt in my mind he was hoping I have some interest.

And I do.

I didn't want to but as Colt walked Linnie and me down to my car once it had gotten dark, he waited until Linnie shut the passenger door, and put his hand out on the driver's door, which prevented me from opening it up.

"Would you like to go out to dinner with me Friday night? I'd like to take you to Clementine's on a date."

His request was simple and direct, and it completely floored me. I was hesitant when I asked, "What does that mean?"

Colt leaned down, bringing his face closer to mine. "I'm asking to move out of the friend zone, Darby."

"I'm not even divorced yet," I pointed out.

His eyes focused in on me intently. "I don't care. Do you?"

I thought about it a moment and realized I should care, but I really don't. But I couldn't give him the answer he wanted just then. "I have to worry about Linnie and what she thinks about this. Her father is still putting on a hard press with her to convince me to come home. I think she still has hopes it's going to happen."

Colt took a slight step back to put a little bit of distance between us. His voice was soft and unassuming. "I'm not moving in, and I'm not asking you to marry me. I'm just asking you out to dinner. But I get you should probably talk to Linnie about this first. You just let me know."

I couldn't have been more appreciative of his low-pressure pitch.

I've never known how to be anything other than truthful with my daughter. Sure, she's only seven and some truths have to be carefully worded so she understands them, but I wasn't about to change my philosophy on how to parent her at this time. I merely brought it up as we drove home that evening. "Linnie… Colt asked me out to dinner one night. And I want to know what you think about it?"

I didn't realize how hard I was gripping the steering wheel until the ends of my fingertips started tingling. When I glanced over at Linnie, she gave me a short look. "I guess it's okay."

"I want to make sure, because I know you still want your daddy and me to get back together."

Linnie almost caused me to run off the road with her next words. "I don't want that anymore."

I gave her a sharp look before focusing back on the road. I was very careful with my next words. "That's kind of a big change of heart you've had."

She didn't say anything at first, but then her words were soft—almost a whisper—as if she was ashamed to admit. "Colt made me think. He asked me if I wanted you to be happy, and I do. I think you'll never be happy with Dad."

I reached my hand out and squeezed her leg. "No, honey. I would never be happy with Dad."

"And it's not so bad here," Linnie added, pushing her glasses up her nose." Because Colt is going to arrange for riding lessons."

I couldn't help but laugh, again realizing just another reason why I am immensely intrigued by and attracted to Colt. He went above and beyond to give my daughter something she loves.

So that's how in a matter of five days—from Sunday supper to Friday night—I am on a date with Colt Mancinkus.

And let me just say I've seen Colt wearing everything from faded jeans to frayed shorts, but the man dressed up is absolutely lethal. His longish hair seems to be styled, but not. As if he had run his fingers through the waves and they settled in the perfect position. He has on a pair of charcoal-gray dress pants with black oxfords and a French blue button-down shirt. He didn't wear a suit jacket, but I assume this is probably as dressy as Clementine's gets.

I don't mind Colt's hand on my lower back as he guides me into the restaurant and tells the woman standing at the podium in the front that he has reservations. We're led back to a small table set for two up against a wall that's glowing with candlelight and crisp linens. Colt holds my chair out for me, which tells me he's much more than just a farm boy.

After we get settled in, we give our drink orders to the waiter and peruse our menus. I order the scallops and Colt a thick ribeye. We both munch on an appetizer of fried calamari and chitchat about a variety of different things.

Colt tells me all about his buddy, Travis, who has opened his barn for Linnie to come riding anytime she wants. As it stands, we're going to start her out three days a week after school, and the cost is well within my budget. If it looks like we're going to stick around, I'll either arrange to have her horse brought down from Illinois if I can talk Mitch into paying for it or perhaps we can buy her one down here.

Our meals come, and they look absolutely divine. My experience with Whynot food has been good, of course. Central Café is the perfect diner, and Larkin's bakery is unparalleled. I've even enjoyed a frozen pizza at Pap's for lunch one day when I came into town to do some grocery shopping.

But Clementine's?

It could hold its own with some of the finest restaurants at which I've eaten in. My honey-broiled scallops are cooked to perfection, and Colt's steak is mouthwatering in appearance. He offers me a bite, and my suspicions that it's a perfect steak are confirmed.

We eat slowly, and the conversation turns a little more personal. I learn Colt is twenty-eight, which is three years younger than me. He's never been in a serious relationship, and by serious, he defined that as wanting to settle down with one woman for the rest of his life. He gives me a charming smile and says, "It doesn't mean I'm not looking, though."

There are definite butterflies in my stomach, but I actually have to remind myself I need to move slowly no matter how perfect he seems to be.

"Can I ask you a personal question?" Colt asks as he sets his utensils down and wipes his mouth with his napkin.

"Sure." I also dab my lips. After placing my napkin back on my lap, I take a sip of the wine he ordered.

"Why did your marriage end?" His question is blunt. Not in a judgmental way but in a way that tells me he's having a tough time reconciling the Darby he's come to know with the one stuck in a bad marriage.

I take another sip of my wine and set it down. I consider for a moment giving him a very glossed-over version, but I toss away that thought just as quickly. Even though the circumstances that led me into a bad marriage are embarrassing, I'm not ashamed to share that information with Colt.

"I imagine you must think I'm a strong and independent woman who is not afraid to take on the world," I begin by saying.

He smirks. "You think pretty highly of yourself, don't you?"

I laugh, but then he's telling me, "Yeah. That's exactly what I see so it's hard for me to understand how you could have been kept under someone's thumb."

I nod in understanding. I am a different person today than I was yesterday. "When I met Mitch, I was fresh out of college and had just started working for the same company as him. He was eleven years older and an executive there. We sort of had this whirlwind romance and I'm not going to lie, he swept me off my feet. Flowers every day, fancy dinners, sparkling jewelry, and expensive trips."

"Dang... I'd like to marry him," Colt jokes as if he senses I need to keep this light.

I stifle a giggle. "It was overwhelming to me. And I fell for it. Fell in love with him. He was smart, charming, and attentive. When he asked me to marry him, I had absolutely no hesitation. He was everything I wanted."

I try to disregard the uncomfortable look on Colt's face and push forward with my story. "I don't know if I had stars in my eyes or I was just so eager to give him what he wanted since he seemed to be giving me everything I wanted, that when he wanted to have a kid right away, I said yes. When Linnie was born, and he wanted me to be a stay-at-home mother, I said yes. And for a while, it was all good. I loved being a homemaker and a mother, and I loved devoting my attention to my family."

Colt puts his forearms on the edge of the table and leans closer, his eyes rapt with attention. "But that changed."

I nod. "Especially when Linnie started school. I figured it was a good time for me to get back into the workforce and finish my degree. But Mitch just always seemed to have a reason why I shouldn't do that. He wanted me to be home when Linnie got home from school. He wanted me to be available to travel with him. He wanted me to throw fancy dinner parties in the middle of the week. All of that was to help further his career, or so he said."

Colt's expression is a mix of disgust and wonder. "He sounds kind of old-fashioned."

"Exactly. Like really old-fashioned. Mitch wanted a wife who would greet him at the front door with his slippers, a pipe, and a highball glass filled with two fingers of scotch. He would then go rest in his recliner while I finished the perfect dinner and helped Linnie with her homework after I cleaned the kitchen. I felt like I was living in the fifties. And suddenly... I didn't want that anymore."

"Your dreams had gotten put aside and you were ready to

pursue them again. I imagine that caused some tension."

"It was horrible. We were fighting constantly. I was trying to push back at him, and he was pushing back ten times as hard at me. I had made up my mind I wanted out of the marriage, but I wasn't quite sure how to go about doing it. I guess there's always the fear I couldn't make it on my own. Or perhaps I was fearful it would be too traumatizing to Linnie. I always seem to have one excuse or another and months and then years would just creep by. So much time wasted."

"So what made you take the leap?" he asks me softly.

"I found out he had a mistress. He was paying for a fancy apartment and a brand-new BMW for her. And I wasn't really pissed off he was sleeping with someone else, but it was insulting as hell that she had a newer car than I did."

Colt throws back his head and laughs so loud several people turn to look at us. I can't help but join him because I've always been a big believer in finding the humor in dark situations.

After my chuckling winds down, I take another sip of wine. "That really gave me the strength to make the break. I guess I always felt foolish leaving a marriage because I wanted to pursue my dreams. It didn't seem so foolish when I found out my husband was cheating on me."

Colt leans back in his seat and picks up his wineglass. He stares at it thoughtfully for a moment before holding it up in a toast. "I think things happened exactly the way they were supposed to happen for you, Darby. And I think you've done a fantastic job so far. Cheers."

I hold my glass out and we lightly tap them, the soft clink making me smile.

I'm not going to lie; my heart feels very full right now by knowing Colt has validated me and my decisions.

CHAPTER 14

Colt

I BEND OVER the counter, watching as Floyd meticulously fills in an order form for me. All the grapevines have been planted, and we're in the process of finishing the drip irrigation installation. As always seems to happen with any type of project like this, we end up busting a few bolts or stripping a few screws. I had to run into town to purchase those while the crew continued to work. I also needed to put in a volume order of timbers, wire, and such to build a few more trellises. I'm going to plant another acre of grapes because I had a little bit of funds left over from the expansion grant.

The front of Floyd's Hardware Emporium is a large pane of glass that looks out over the Courthouse Square. Floyd's back is to the window, but movement across the way catches my attention.

My pulse picks up when I spy Darby and Linnie walking into Sweet Cakes.

"Why do you have that goofy smile on your face?" Floyd asks, and I bring my eyes back to him to find him staring at me thoughtfully. My eyes cut back over his shoulder as I watch Darby disappear into the bakery. Floyd looks over his shoulder and then back to me with raised eyebrows.

"Hurry up and finish that order, buddy," I instruct him. I pull out my wallet and fish out the Mainer Farms credit card.

"I've got things to do."

"You've got a girl to run after," Floyd says confidently.

My goofy smile gets goofier.

I'm not surprised by the smile on my face. It's been there since I woke up this morning. I've been on a lot of first dates over my lifetime. Sometimes they can be stressful, sometimes they can be fun. If it's a good date, it will leave me with a smile on my face the next day.

Last night, dinner with Darby was beyond just a "good" date. It was amazing and has produced a big, goofy smile today.

I'm not a confirmed bachelor or anything. I look at my parents' marriage, and I want that. I see how much happier my sister Trixie is with Ry, Lowe is with Mely, and Laken is with Jake. Like dominoes, all the Mancinkus kids seem to be falling in love. I honestly don't know if that's what is going to happen between Darby and me, but I can tell she is different from any other woman I have dated.

We stayed at Clementine's last night for almost three hours, and they actually had to run us out of the restaurant. We sat there after the wine was finished, and I drink some sweet tea while she sipped a sparkling water. We talked, and talked, and talked. We moved on from the heavy subject matter of her marriage and hopped around topics such as political leanings and religious beliefs.

Sometimes we talked about silly stuff like most embarrassing moments or favorite movies. We spent a lot of time talking about Jake, and this was good since I suspect he's going to be proposing to my sister before too long. Darby knows him extremely well, and I was able to snoop around as a brother should in protection of his sister. It turns out, as I suspected, that Jake is a good guy and I was relieved.

I took Darby back to Farrington Farms after we left the restaurant. It was going on close to eleven o'clock by the time we pulled in. Because I am southern and my mama taught me the right way, I walked Darby up the porch to the front door. Jake's car and Laken's truck were in the driveway, and the lights were on in the living room. I could see the glow coming through the frosted glass panes of the door. They were on Linnie-sitting duty tonight.

Darby turned to face me and for the first time that night, there was a tiny bit of an awkward moment.

To go in for the kiss or not?

I absolutely wanted to kiss Darby. I could tell by the look on her face she would've let me. Instead, I let my instinct guide me and I took her hand in mine. Pulling it up to my mouth, I pressed my lips against her knuckles briefly and then gave her a smile as I released her. "Good night, Darby. I had a wonderful time."

She blinked at me for a moment, somewhat surprised I didn't kiss her on the mouth. I could also tell she was amused and that she liked the fact I only kissed her hand.

Yeah… it's going to be a slow burn if we are going to burn at all. And I think we will. That's fine by me, taking it slow. Before Darby walked into my life, I was not particularly looking for a relationship. I wasn't avoiding one, but my main priority was Mainer Farms. It's still my priority, but the fact Darby and I have so much in common when it comes to our careers and livelihood makes me realize there could be room for more.

I wonder if Darby is the "more" I need.

Floyd finishes the order form and I scrawl my name on it. It seems to take forever for him to run my credit card, as he requires a fifty percent deposit on such orders. After he hands it back to me, I shove it in my wallet and hightail it out of the hardware store. I trot across the street, Courthouse Square, and the next street, coming to a stop at the door to Sweet Cakes.

Taking a deep breath in, I let it out and open the door. Darby and Linnie are standing at the bakery case and both turn to look at me. I take a moment to notice Darby's eyes widen and then twinkle with happiness to see me.

That feels really, really good.

But my attention is taken away by Linnie exclaiming, "Colt."

I'm almost bowled over backward when she flies at me and throws her arms around my waist. I didn't take Linnie for an outwardly affectionate kid, but I am not displeased when she hugs the hell out of me.

My gaze slides over to Darby, and I find her frowning as she watches Linnie. Not in an unhappy way but more in a contemplative one that shows me she's as surprised by Linnie's behavior as I am. But then that look melts away and she gives me a welcoming smile.

Linnie releases me, and I look back to Darby. "Saw you two walk in here. Thought I would come by and say hello."

At that moment, Larkin comes in from the back and smiles at all of us. "Well, look at this crowd hanging out in my store this morning."

"We want to get a birthday cake ordered for Carlos. His thirty-seventh birthday is on Wednesday."

"And some chocolate chip cookies," Linnie adds. Darby laughs as she puts her arms around her daughter to give her a squeeze.

She looks to Larkin and nods, "And half a dozen chocolate chip cookies."

I step up to the counter and pull my wallet out, fishing out a twenty and handing it to Larkin. "The cookies are on me."

"Thank you kindly," Darby says as she bats her eyes and lowers her chin coyly.

I laugh in response and watch as Linnie rolls her eyes. Larkin fishes out the chocolate chip cookies, handing one across the counter to Linnie and putting the rest in a pink bag. She takes my money and gives me back my change.

The tinkling bells over the door erupt, and we all turn to see Della Padgett walking in. She owns a bookstore beside Floyd's hardware store. It's called The Reader's Nook, and I like to go there on occasion to buy the latest thriller that might be out.

The first thing I notice about Della when she walks in is the extraordinarily huge smile on her face.

"You clearly have some good news," Larkin observes from behind the counter.

Without any preamble, Della is holding out her hand and sticking it right in my face. I pull my head back so she doesn't pop me on the nose, but she's already spinning from me and sticking her hand up to Larkin's face.

Larkin gasps and takes Della's hand in both of her own. I then realize she's admiring a diamond ring Della is showing off.

"Oh my God," Larkin practically squeals. "Jason popped the question"

Della nods her head furiously. "Just last night. We were at Clementine's. He just got down on his knee and proposed to me right there in the middle of the restaurant."

Darby and I shoot a glance at each other, and she shrugs. Neither one of us saw that last night.

As if she could read our silent exchange, Della turns and studies us. "I saw you two there having dinner. But you were so caught up in each other you didn't even notice Jason proposing to me."

Darby's face flushes red, and I have to bite the inside of my cheek not to laugh. But it's true. The restaurant probably could have burned down around us, and I doubt Darby and I would have noticed.

Darby steps up to Della, holding her hand out in a silent request to check out the engagement ring. Della is only too happy to comply and puts her plump hand in Darby's. I have to admit, Jason didn't skimp on the diamond. It's big and flashy. But Jason's got a good business. He owns the gas station here in Whynot, which also has a wine shop incorporated within that's quite successful. He's not hurting for money.

"The ring is just beautiful," Darby says as she admires the rock. "Oh, by the way... I'm Darby. That's my daughter Linnie."

Della turns her hand so she and Darby are now shaking. "So very good to meet you. I've actually heard lots about the pretty peach farmer who moved into town."

She then shoots me a sly look and adds, "And you and Colt Mancinkus dating. Isn't that just wonderful?"

My eyes cut to Linnie to see her reaction to this very public proclamation that Darby and I are dating, though I'm not sure we are.

Maybe we are.

I don't know.

Linnie just stares back at me as she munches on her chocolate chip cookie. She even gives me a tiny smile in the form of one side of her mouth quirking upward.

Darby had told me that she had talked to Linnie about us going out to dinner, and Linnie said she was fine with it. I'm guessing she really is fine with it.

Della spins back toward Larkin and places the palms of her hand on the short counter where the cash register rests. "I just came in so I can put in the order for a wedding cake. We're not going to do anything big. Probably just have Judge Bowe marry us at the courthouse and then a party at the train depot. Lots of tasty food. Of course, we'll have the most wonderful wedding cake in the world done by my dear friend, Larkin Mancinkus."

Larkin starts shaking her head and holds her hands up, palms out toward Della. "I can't do a wedding cake. I've never done a wedding cake."

"Well now's your chance to try," Della says matter-of-factly. "You're so talented and creative. I know you can do a pretty cake for me."

Larkin keeps shaking her head and takes a step backward. "No way. I'm not going to be responsible for ruining a wedding."

This doesn't surprise me. Larkin went out on a limb when she decided to open her bakery five years ago. But that's about as far out on a limb as she has gone. She bakes the things she is comfortable with and knows she is very good at. People always find the same things here day in and day out. I'm not surprised she doesn't feel comfortable doing a wedding cake.

I step up to the case and rest my elbow on the top glass. "Larkin... give it a shot. You can practice. If you can't do it, Della can find someone else."

Larkin shoots me a look that is a mixture of panic and loathing that I'm pushing her into this. My sweet sister doesn't like leaving her comfort zone.

Too bad.

She needs to learn to live a little.

"That's a fantastic idea," Della exclaims. She turns and starts for the door, calling over her shoulder, "I'm going to email you some ideas. A few pictures I was looking at last night."

And just like that, Della is gone, and Larkin is on the hook for a wedding cake.

She turns and shoots me a sour look. "How could you do that to me, Colt?"

I shrug and give her an innocent look. "I have no clue what you're talking about."

Larkin huffs and glares.

"Why don't you give it a try, Larkin?" Darby asks her curiously. "I'll come help you experiment. You can try your cakes out on me."

Larkin lets out a tiny huff of capitulation and says, "I guess it couldn't hurt to try. I've got all the decorating equipment I would need."

The door to Sweet Cakes flies open, the bells chiming merrily. Della pokes her head back in and pins a stare on Larkin. "By the way, we're looking at doing the weekend after next."

Larkin's mouth drops open in disbelief.

"Toodles," Della calls out as she disappears, and the door swings shut.

Larkin shoots another loathsome glare at me for getting her roped into this and then an apologetic look at Darby. "I hope you have some time soon because we're going to have to start making cakes."

"I'm ready whenever you are. I mean, it's not a chore to try out cakes."

"The bakery is closed tomorrow," Larkin says. "I'll just forgo dinner at Mama's as I'll probably be working on this all day."

"Do you have to do everything here or want to do it at my house?" Darby asks. "That way Linnie can entertain herself if she gets bored with us."

Larkin shakes her head. "I can bake the cakes here, and we can decorate at your house. How does that sound? I'll just do several six-inch rounds to practice on."

"Awesome," Darby says exuberantly. "And I'll cook dinner for us if we run into the evening, although we might be full of cake."

I can't help but smile over the fast friendship forming between my sister and Darby. Not only because Larkin has always been a bit of a loner because she works so much, but also because that means Darby is putting down additional roots here.

Turning those pretty blue eyes my way, Darby offers, "If you can do without Sunday dinner at your mom's, you're more than welcome to come eat with us?"

"Yeah, you can hang out with us all day to decorate cakes," Larkin quips.

I shake my head and nip that right in the bud. "No way. I do not decorate cakes."

"I don't want to decorate cakes, either," Linnie says. She turns hopeful eyes my way. "Think we could go ride horses together instead?"

I laugh and ruffle the top of Linnie's hair. She pulls away from me with a grimace.

But I shoot her a wink and say, "Sounds like fun."

Then I turn to Darby and add, "And I'd be glad to join y'all for dinner."

"It's a date then," Darby says, but immediately flushes as she stammers, "Well, it's not a date-date. Just that... well, you know."

I think it's adorable she gets flustered talking about a date, and it brings something to mind. My hand shoots out and snatches her by the wrist. I look at Larkin and then to Linnie, making an apology as I drag Darby to the front door. "I need to steal your mother for a moment. Be right back."

I have a glimpse of Linnie biting down into her chocolate chip cookie, and I can hear Larkin snort as we step out onto the sidewalk.

I turn to face Darby, and she's looking at me with an expectant smile on her face. "What's up?"

"Well," I say slyly as I step into her. "When I saw you from Floyd's Hardware Emporium a little bit ago, I came over to see you with the idea in mind of asking you out on another date."

She sidles in a tiny bit closer and asks in a sweet voice, "Oh yeah?"

"Yeah," I murmur. "Figure I can't get to the first kiss without another date."

Darby gives a husky laugh even as her cheeks turn a little pink. "I would love to go out on another date with you, Colt."

"Well, that works out well for both of us then, doesn't it?"

She gives me a saucy wink in return before she opens the door to step back into Sweet Cakes. "That it does. And thanks for the cookies for Linnie by the way. See you tomorrow."

CHAPTER 15

Darby

J AKE AND I crest the hill, and the gray Farrington barn comes into view. I had walked him out to show him the progress on the peach orchard. We decided to hoof it rather than use the Gator as it was a beautiful day and we had nothing but time.

The goat pasture is on our left, and both Linnie and Laken are in there. Laken came out to trim the goat's hooves today and asked Linnie if she wanted to learn how. I wasn't all that surprised when she said she did. Linnie absolutely loves animals. While she doesn't have any experience with them other than her horse, I don't think she's afraid to get her hands dirty with farm life. This makes me incredibly happy, of course.

"So all the holes should be finished today," I tell Jake as we walk toward the barn.

I had hired a man with a backhoe and an auger attachment to dig all the holes for the rootstock trees. Because Jake has an endless supply of money and wants to operate at a loss, I made the decision to go ahead and purchase peach trees that had been nursery raised for two years. That would give us a bit of a head start on production.

"They're going to be delivered on Monday, and I have a crew of almost thirty who will be here to help."

Jake nods as we trudge along. He's transformed from the

polished Chicago businessman into a farmer himself. He's got on a pair of faded jeans and work boots caked with soil and red clay. "How many trucks is it going to take to get them in?"

"I think the guy said at least five full-sized flatbeds," I say vaguely. The nursery owner had told me that information, but it wasn't overly important, so I can't quite remember. "He's going to stagger the deliveries though throughout the day.

I had to arrange for a few tractors with flatbed trailers to be ready for when the trees would arrive. The tractor-trailers hauling them in wouldn't be able to turn off the highway into Farrington Farms. There is absolutely no way they're going to make it over the farm road to where the orchard was located. So the crew of people would be here to unload the trees onto the tractor flatbeds, and we would drive them out to the orchard for unloading. It's a labor-intensive process but again, Jake pretty much gave me an open checkbook and told me to do it the most efficient way possible.

Oh, to have that type of money.

"I am so darned impressed with you, Darby," Jake murmurs as we walk side by side. "I can't believe how fast you got this up and running."

"Thanks," I say as I beam on the inside. "But I did a lot of the pre-work while I was still living in Illinois."

"Still, you have transitioned very seamlessly. I'm proud of you, sis."

A warm bubbling fills me up over his use of the word "sis". Even though he and Kelly are no longer married, I still consider him to be my brother. It's nice to know he feels the same about me.

"How are things going with Mitch?" he asks me, the concern in his voice evident.

I stumble over the unexpected question, and Jake latches onto my elbow until I steady. He chuckles and reprimands me, "Come on, Darby. You had to have known I'm going to keep my nose in your business."

I laugh, and he releases my elbow. "I know. We were just having such a nice talk and you had to bring him into it. It took me by surprise."

Jake laughs again, but then his expression sobers. "Seriously… how are things going?"

I sigh and shrug at the same time. "It was rough when we first came here. Mitch kept using Linnie as a pawn to try to get me to go back to him. He kept her completely riled up and pissed off at me, but at least that doesn't seem to be working anymore."

"But I sense there's more to the story?" Jake asks. He's always been a perceptive man.

My eyes dart across the field to Linnie, who is helping to hold the goats while Laken works on them. "He's still harassing me. Calls and nasty texts. Our attorneys have been battling things out, but he just won't agree to anything. Then he demands things that just aren't doable."

"Like what?"

"Like his last demand was he would give me full custody if I would agree to bring Linnie to Illinois every other weekend. That's just not feasible. I don't have the time nor the money to do that."

Jake stops in his tracks suddenly and turns to face me. He crosses his arms over his chest, his expression turning very serious. "It sounds to me like he's stalling. Trying to drag this out and maybe making it so difficult on you that you'll just give in."

I look back to Linnie for a moment and then turn my

attention to Jake's observation. "I think you're exactly right. I just don't understand why he won't give me up. I mean, come on, Jake… The guy has a mistress. Those needs are being seen to. He can marry somebody else to cook for him and clean his house. Why is he still focused on me?"

Jake's arms drop, and his hands come to my shoulders for a reassuring squeeze. "I suspect he thinks he still loves you. And let's face it, the man always had horrible self-esteem along with an oddly inflated ego. One of the best things you ever did for him was pump up his ego on a daily basis."

I blink in surprise. "Excuse me?"

Jake makes a clucking sound with his tongue. "Surely you knew that, Darby. You were a trophy wife for Mitch. You made him feel good about himself. I guarantee you he's quite lost without the perfect little wife to run his household and make him feel all manly and such."

I cannot control the shudder that ripples up my spine because in that context, it just sounds extremely creepy Mitch would need that from me. Regardless, it doesn't give me any insight on how to deal with him.

"Listen," he says to get my attention focused on him. "I don't want you to have to stoop down to the games he's playing. I think you need to let your attorney get very nasty with him. He was cheating on you and that gives you leverage in the divorce settlement."

"I know," I tell him with frustration. "But there's only so much I can afford to pay this attorney to do."

"Then let me clarify what I'm saying," Jake says with a smirk. "I'm going to give you my checkbook. You have carte blanche to write any amount to your attorney that will get you to prevail in the divorce settlement. You tell your attorney you want it done quickly and without any mercy."

I can't help it. I throw my head back and start laughing, then I double over and hold my stomach while I laugh even harder. I manage to look up through tears of mirth to find Jake glaring at me. It makes me laugh even more hysterically.

Jake's arms go back over his chest, and he waits out my amusement.

When I'm done, he asks, "Why do you find that so funny?"

"You are my former brother-in-law, Jake," I say with a snort. "I'm not going to take your money to fund my divorce."

Jake's face crumbles, and he looks hurt by my words. He gives a shake of his head and his tone is chiding. "Darby... I still consider you family. I thought you felt the same for me."

I start shaking my head and wagging my finger at him. "Oh no you don't. You don't get to pull that family crap on me just so I'll use your money."

"Did you know I make almost seven million a year just in salary and stock options?" he asks me smoothly.

I blink like an owl at him.

"And did you know that my net worth is close to forty-two million?"

I shake my head, my lips and tongue completely numb with shock.

"You're going to take my blank check and fund your divorce, Darby," Jake says in a domineering tone. "I can afford it. And if you don't do it, I'm going to fire you as the operations manager for Farrington Farms. Now you and Linnie are more than welcome to stay here rent free after I fire you, but you're not going to have that nice little title of operations manager and you're not gonna have any say so over this peach orchard. And then how will you finish your thesis?

So you can call it bribery or you can call it strong-arming or whatever, but you're going to do this. It will give me peace of mind because I still love you and Linnie very much."

I can do nothing but stare silently at my former brother-in-law who is very much like a real brother to me in every sense of the word. I open my mouth, but no words come out.

The only thing I can do is throw my arms around his shoulders to give him a hard hug of acceptance. I bite down into my lips so I don't start crying.

Jake's arms come around me, and he gives me a squeeze in return before releasing me.

We continue our walk toward the barn, Jake lapsing back into questions about the orchard.

As we approach, Linnie and Laken come walking out of the goat pasture. Laken holds the gate open far enough for little MG to slip through and she runs up to Jake, her tail wagging a hundred miles an hour.

I don't think I've ever been as charmed as I was to learn this sweet little goat bonded with Jake shortly after she was born. For weeks, she refused to drink from her mother or from anyone else other than Jake. It's one of the things that precipitated him spending more time here, which in turn led to him getting to know Laken better.

Therefore, Miss Goatikins is directly responsible for bringing Jake and Laken together. While the little kid has grown up some and is asserting more independence, she still goes crazy anytime she sees Jake. He leans down when she puts her front hooves up on his knee and picks her up. He holds her with one arm supporting underneath her belly, his hand spread wide across her chest. He tucks her in close to his side. Her little tail is visible underneath his armpit, and it's still wagging mercilessly as she butts her head against his jaw.

Cutest damn thing I've ever seen.

"Mom," Linnie says excitedly with a tiny push of her glasses up her nose. "Laken actually let me do some of the trimming."

I blink at Linnie in surprise, turning to Laken with a cocked eyebrow.

Laken shrugs. "What can I say? Your kid is a natural when it comes to caring for the goats. I'm glad you decided to keep them."

I bring my gaze back to Linnie with a soft smile, chuck her under the chin, and tell her, "I'm proud of you, baby. And I'm really glad you're taking to the goats."

"I don't know about you ladies, but I am starting to get really hungry," Jake says as he scratches MG's head. "I was thinking about riding over to Milner and picking up some pizza for us. How does that sound?"

The sun is starting to drop fast, and we have spent most of the day outside. We had some bologna sandwiches for lunch, but I could definitely be down with some pizza tonight. "Sounds good to me."

"Me too," Laken adds on. "Want me to ride with you, babe?"

Jake shakes his head and grins at Linnie. "Want to go with me, kiddo? You haven't hung out with your Uncle Jake in a while."

She rolls her eyes. "I just spent last night with you and Laken when Mom went out to dinner with Colt."

Jake shakes his head and gives her a stern look. "No, you pretty much spent the entire evening hanging out with Laken. In fact, you both ignored me. So how about riding with me to Milner to go pick up the pizza?"

Linnie gives a dramatic eye roll with a long-suffering sigh. "Fine. I'll go with you."

Chuckling, Jake turns to Laken and unloads the tiny goat into her arms. He leans over and gives her a hard peck on her cheek and a swat on her butt. "We'll be back soon."

Laken walks back to the pasture and opens the fence to set MG inside. As she comes out, she gives me a pointed look. "I could use a beer. How about you?"

Within moments, we are inside. After we wash our hands and pull cold bottles of beer from the refrigerator, we head back out to the porch and sit on the top step while we wait for Jake and Linnie to return with the pizza. It's starting to get chilly, but I'm still warm from the long hike we had out to the orchard and back.

We're both silent as we sip on our beer and stare out at the goat pasture. That doesn't last long, though, because Laken breaks the silence by asking, "So, how was your date last night?"

I twist my neck to look at her. It's uncanny how much all the Mancinkus kids look like each other with their dark hair and beautiful hazel eyes. Turning to gaze back out over the goat pasture, I say, "It was really nice."

"Oh, hell no," she exclaims and gives me a tiny punch to my arm. "I need more details."

Chuckling and rubbing my arm, I admit, "Your brother is really great. I like him a lot, and I feel terrible I like him so much."

Laken pulls back from me in surprise. "Why would you say that?"

I take a slug of my beer and wipe my mouth with the back of my hand. "Because I'm not even divorced yet. I just got out of a terrible marriage. The last thing in the world I should be doing is getting involved with a man. I don't even think I'm being fair to Colt."

"Colt is a grown man. He doesn't seem to have any problems with your situation."

I give Laken an exasperated look. "I know he doesn't. But I do. It doesn't seem, well… seemly. I mean, what must Linnie be thinking that I've gone out on a date with a man only three months after separating from her father?"

"Well, what does Linnie think about it? She didn't say anything to Jake and me last night, but she was not bent out of shape at all."

"She seems fine with it," I say softly, stubbornly refusing to accept the fact Laken just removed that worry. "But well, what will everyone else think?"

Laken chuckles, and then gives me a friendly nudge with her shoulder. "I can tell you the Mancinkus clan likes it a lot. We all adore you and Linnie, and Colt clearly likes you. Quit thinking about things so much and just go with the flow."

"Go with the flow? That's your advice?"

Laken turns slightly so her knees bump into mine and she can look me in the eye. "Darby, I am quite confident you would not intentionally hurt my brother. I think you're sweet and funny and kind and brilliant. I also think you are perfect for someone like Colt and he's perfect for someone like you. Take your time with it if you want. Stick to a friendship if it makes you feel better. But don't get scared and do nothing. You've got a fantastic opportunity in front of you, and I'm not saying that just because I think my brother is the cat's meow."

I can't help but laugh over her declaration, and I am completely overwhelmed by the relief I feel by getting this validation from Laken.

More than anything, I am glad to hear her say the things she did, because no matter how weird it may seem given I've only been separated for three months, I really want to see where this goes.

CHAPTER 16

Colt

I T'S PRACTICALLY A zoo when I pull up to Farrington Farms Monday afternoon. I knew Darby would be elbow deep in the planting of the peach trees. All the holes had been dug in the prior days with a large auger, and she had tractor-trailers bringing in ten-acres worth of two-year-old nursery-raised peach trees today. There was a good chance I would be doing nothing more than getting in her hair with my visit.

Didn't stop me, though.

The pasture on the opposite side of the gravel driveway that leads up to the main house is filled with several vehicles, mostly trucks. I assume those are the temporary workers Darby hired. There is a large flatbed tractor-trailer taking up the entire eastbound lane of the highway that runs perpendicular to the farm road. It's completely empty. The workers look to be transferring the last load of trees onto a tractor with a flatbed cart attached to it, which will then transport the trees out to the orchard.

I see Darby immediately, looking as fetching as ever. She's got on a heavy flannel shirt, jeans, and work boots. She's got her strawberry-blonde hair in a ponytail with a baseball cap on her head. Pointing to some of the workers, she seems to be giving them instructions regarding the trees.

I'm not sure what it is about a woman in charge and running her own farm that makes her singularly attractive to me, but Darby McCulhane pushes every one of my buttons. I grab the bunch of wildflowers off the passenger seat of my truck and hop out. Making my way toward her, I watch as she effortlessly directs people to do different things. When I get just a few feet from her, it's as if she can sense my presence, and she turns toward me with a smile already in place.

Her eyes cut to the flowers in my hand and then back to my face.

"What are you doing here?" she chirps as she walks my way, that ponytail bouncing back and forth because of the pep in her step.

"Well, seeing as how my entire vineyard has been planted and there's nothing left to do but some minor irrigation modifications, I thought I would come hang out with you this afternoon and watch how a peach orchard gets started." I hold the flowers out to her, and she takes them. "And here are some wildflowers I stopped to pick from the side of the road."

It's so cute when Darby lifts the loose bouquet to her nose and breathes them in deeply. I don't think they smell all that spectacular, but they were so pretty on the side of the road I couldn't resist. She gives a dreamy sigh and opens her eyes to stare at me. "Now that's romantic."

I give a careless shrug as if I do romantic stuff all the time. I don't, but I think I will be starting based on her reaction. "So how's it going today?"

She jerks her chin over her shoulder toward the tractor-trailer. "That's the last load. All the trees have been laid out near the holes, and the crew will come back tomorrow morning to start the planting."

My eyes cut out to the highway before coming back to Darby. "Is Linnie home from school yet?"

Darby shakes her head and glances down at her watch.

"Not yet but she should be soon."

I reach out and take Darby's free hand. She blinks in surprise but doesn't hesitate in giving it to me. I give her a devilish smile and say, "Before she gets here, I wanted to see if I could secure another date with you. Didn't get much of a chance yesterday during all that cake making you were doing and dinner with Larkin and Linnie watching."

Darby laughs. "What did you have in mind?"

"I thought I would take you and Linnie to the North Carolina State fair in Raleigh this weekend," I tell her.

Darby's mouth falls slightly open for a moment. She shakes her head and gives me a wry smile. "Thought you were asking me out on a date?"

"Then let me clarify. This is sort of a date with you and your daughter. I remember you telling me at dinner the other night that you hated amusement park rides while I, on the other hand, love them. I also know your little girl is a daredevil so I would like to bring her with us so she can ride all the rides with me. But I promise I'll win you a big stuffed animal. I'm actually really good with the balloons and darts."

Darby laughs and shakes her head with amusement. "You are just too much, Colt Mancinkus. How could a woman ever say no to that offer?"

My heart leaps, and I'm filled with giddiness at the thought of spending a full day with Darby. Even with her daughter along, I know I'm going to have an awesome time. How could I not when both Darby and Linnie are simply two awesome people?

I pull her hand up to my mouth and give it a kiss just the way I did when I walked her to her door after our first date. Walking backward toward my truck, I say, "I'll pick both of you up Saturday morning about nine."

She grins back at me. "I can't wait."

At that moment, the grinding gears and squeaky brakes of a school bus have both Darby and me turning to look toward the highway. It's almost like deja vu as Linnie gets off the bus and trudges up the lane toward us with her head lowered, staring at the ground. I can tell by the hunch to her shoulders that she didn't have a particularly good day.

I'm not sure whether Linnie sees us, but she tries to walk by without even raising her head.

Darby takes a step toward her and calls, "Hey Linnie... How was school today?"

Linnie mutters what I think was the word "good" but doesn't look up and continues to walk by us.

Darby moves fast. She jogs just a couple of paces and takes Linnie's arm in her hand, gently turning her around. Linnie still won't look up, so Darby puts her fingers under her daughter's chin to lift her face.

Darby gasps just as my blood heats to boiling as we both take in the dark purple bruising underneath Linnie's right eye.

"Oh my God," Darby exclaims. She drops to her knees, which I know had to have hurt given that the lane is made of gravel. When she cups Linnie's face in her hands, she turns her from side to side so she can examine her. "What happened to you?"

I walk up to stand behind Darby, looking down at a little girl sporting a shiner I can tell will probably only be worse come tomorrow.

Linnie's blue eyes fill with tears, and she gives a tiny push of her glasses up her nose. "I got in a fight."

"A fight?" Darby asks softly, her tone attempting to coax the necessary information from her daughter.

Linnie pushes her glasses up again as she mutters, "I got in the way of Caleb's fist."

"That boy you said was bullying you?" Darby snarls in outrage.

I can feel my blood pressure start to rise as I think about that little brat punching Linnie. He's way bigger than she is, and boys don't punch girls.

"If you ladies will excuse me," I grit through my teeth. I turn on my heel and start toward my truck. "I'm going to handle this."

"Colt," Darby cries out in worry. I stop and turn to look at her. "Are you going over to that kid's house or something?"

"You're darn right I am," I tell her. My blood continues to boil at a nuclear level. "I'll be back in a little bit."

"But you can't," Darby says, but she doesn't sound quite so sure I can't really do this. "I mean… this is my responsibility."

I sweep my hand toward my truck. "Would you like to go with me?"

"Mom… please don't," Linnie says as she takes her mom's hand. "I really don't feel good, and I just want to go inside."

And just like that, I'm forgotten, as is Caleb Rochelle. Darby bends down and scoops Linnie up. Little arms go around Darby's neck and her legs wrap around her mom's waist. She lays her head on Darby's shoulder. I didn't think it was possible for me to get more mad, but the little sob that comes out of Linnie's mouth has me stomping toward my truck with purpose.

It only takes me about fifteen minutes to drive back to Whynot, through town past Jason's gas station where Caleb's mom Missy works part time. Her car is parked on the side of the building, but I hit the gas. She's not the one I want to talk to anyway. I keep going for another five miles before I turn left onto a dirt road with a sign out front proclaiming it to be Goddard Farms. Last I heard, Jimmy Rochelle was working here. If he's not, I'll try his house next, which is only about another mile down the road.

Goddard Farms is one of the few still left in our area that hasn't leased out any of their land to bigger companies. I'm not sure how they've maintained, but I think it has something to do with the fact they are a small farm and can work it with minimal help. This keeps their overhead down and probably lets them turn a decent profit on the soybeans and field corn they mainly grow.

There's not a typical barn so to speak but rather Mr. Goddard keeps all of his equipment under a massive freestanding structure made of aluminum with no walls. It's basically to keep the rain off. I see Jimmy's little blue Toyota truck with the muffler hanging down parked there. I pull in right behind it and shut off my engine.

Just as I'm slamming my truck door shut, Mr. Goddard himself walks out from behind an old John Deere tractor wiping his hands off with a grease rag. His face lights up when he sees me, and he calls out, "What can I do you for, Colt?"

I give him as pleasant a smile as I can muster, but I can tell by the look on his face he knows I'm not a happy camper. "Is Jimmy Rochelle around?"

"Why?" he asks suspiciously. "You plan on kicking his butt or killing him on my property?"

I give a shake of my head. "No, sir. But I do need to have some words with him."

Mr. Goddard jerks his thumb over his shoulder to a small work shed with the doors propped open. "He's in there cleaning some tools."

I turn to walk that way, but Mr. Goddard calls out to me

again, "How's Pap doing? I haven't had a chance to see him since his surgery."

I take in a breath and let it out slowly, forcing myself to put on a pleasant smile as I face Mr. Goddard. He's a nice old man and he's worried about Pap, so I can take a few minutes to assure him. "He's doing really good. Bounced back from that surgery better than any one of us kids ever would have. You should go down and have a drink with him."

Mr. Goddard shakes his head. "Had to give that stuff up. My liver's been acting up."

I give him a nod of understanding, but I think more than anything Mrs. Goddard has probably put her foot down and said no more late nights at Chesty's.

I wave to Mr. Goddard and take off toward the work shed.

When I step in, I'm relieved to know there's no one else in there but Jimmy. He turns to look at me, a smile starting to bloom on his face, but it doesn't go anywhere when he sees the thunderous look on mine. His lips press into a grim expression. "Colt."

"You son punched a little girl in the eye today at school," I growl.

Because Jimmy is a bully himself and I have long suspected he probably knocks Missy around, I'm not surprised when I don't get any reaction from him. Granted, he doesn't look happy his son was beating up on a little girl, but he doesn't look put out of place either. He doesn't say anything, and that infuriates me.

"I want to know what you're going to do about it?" I ask him pointedly.

"Ain't going to do a damn thing," Jimmy says as he turns his back on me.

Yeah, that's not going to work. My hand claps down on his shoulder, and I turn him back forcefully to look at me.

"Try again," I instruct him. "Assure me what you're going to do to make sure your bully of a son doesn't hit that little girl again."

Jimmy puffs his chest out and lifts his chin. I've got about six inches of height on him, so this is a little comical.

"What's it to you?" he asks belligerently. "What little girl is this? I know you ain't got no young-uns."

"She's the daughter of a friend of mine," I grit out. "Now tell me how you're going to rectify this."

Jimmy stares at me blankly for a moment, but then he shrugs in the most nonchalant of ways that has me itching to join my fist with his jaw. "I'll have a talk with the boy."

I can tell by the tone of his voice he has no intention of doing that. I guarantee he won't say a single thing to his son.

"Just to make sure you impart the right information to your son," I tell Jimmy in a deadly quiet voice. "You make sure he understands that the next time he lays a hand on Linnie McCulhane, I'm gonna come here and I will whip his father's butt. For every black eye he gives her, his daddy's going to get two. He bloodies her nose, Daddy's going to get it twice as bad. Am I making myself clear?"

Jimmy is a bully himself, but there's no way he would ever try to go head to head with me. I once whipped his butt really bad in junior high, so he knows I've got the skills to back up what I'm saying. Jimmy swallows hard and gives an uncertain nod.

I beam a brilliant smile his way. "Excellent," I say with enthusiasm. "I think we have an understanding."

And with that, I turn on my heel and walk out of the shed. I wave goodbye to Mr. Goddard, who's standing just outside the door, and jump back in my truck. I don't think about heading back to Farrington Farms but rather decide to go back and check on the progress at the vineyards.

Before I put my truck in drive, I shoot Darby a text to assure her Linnie is done being bullied by Caleb Rochelle.

CHAPTER 17

Darby

MY PHONE BUZZES from within my purse, indicating a text message. It could be from anyone really, but I hope it's from Colt. Before I can look, though, I want to get settled in with Linnie.

I put my hand on my daughter's shoulder and guide her through the tables in Central Café. After I got her tears dried a bit ago and assured her the black eye was barely noticeable, I offered to take her out for milkshakes for dinner. That always got a smile from her in the past, and today is no different.

When we'd walked in, Muriel waved and called out from behind the counter, "Just sit anywhere. I'll be right over."

Linnie hasn't had the privilege of eating at Central Café, nor has she been able to meet many of the townsfolk since we spend so much time out on the farm. I know we're guaranteed to run into an eclectic mix of people on any given trip into town, and I'm hoping that will also help get her mind off things.

We choose a table that seats four in the very back corner of the restaurant that is bordered on one side by the windows that overlook the street. I help Linnie take off her windbreaker and I remove the light wool shawl I had thrown around me before we left the farm. When I sit down, I reach into my purse and pull out my phone.

It is indeed a text from Colt. *Caleb has been handled. He will not be bothering Linnie anymore.*

The relief that courses through me almost makes me laugh with giddiness. Instead, I shoot a quick text back. *You didn't draw actual blood on a child, did you?*

He sends me back an emoji that's laughing with tears coming out of its eyes. He follows that with, *Let's just say his father and I have come to an understanding.*

I think a few moments on how to respond, but there aren't any right words to express my gratitude. I merely write back, *Thank you, Colt. It means the world to me that you did that.*

My pleasure.

Nothing else comes and I realize I want more. So I text him, *Linnie and I are eating an early dinner at Central Café. Join us if you'd like. My treat.*

His text back is prompt. *Maybe I will.*

Smiling, I set my phone down so I'm not tempted to text him again and grab two of the menus that are sitting in the center of the table in a condiment holder. I only take one and open it up, giving it a quick perusal. I already know Linnie will order a strawberry milkshake, which is her favorite, although I'm going to see if I can talk her into something more substantial. While milkshakes for dinner are a great way to ease frustrations and pain, it's not the ideal meal. Funny I'm being a mom by offering milkshakes for dinner to help my kid on a rough day, and I'm still being a mom by wishing I could get her to eat some leafy greens with it.

Fat chance.

"How about a burger and some fries to go with that milkshake?" I ask her.

Linnie smiles, and my heart trips madly from that tiny gesture. On the best of days, Linnie's smile is the best thing in the world. On her worst days, I feel like I've been handed the sun and the moon when I get one. Her tears just a little bit ago were breaking my heart so this smile is much needed.

"Just French fries," she says to me. "I like to dip them in the milkshake."

"That's gross, baby." I wrinkle my nose, but I'll accept that a potato is at least a vegetable.

Muriel shows up at our table with a pad and a pencil in her hand. She's wearing her standard Central Café uniform, and I introduce her to my daughter. "Linnie, this is Miss Muriel. She owns this restaurant."

Linnie looks up and gives her a shy smile, followed by a little push of her glasses up her nose.

Muriel clucks her tongue and shakes her head as she looks at Linnie. "Oh baby, that shiner looks like it smarts. I can't believe that Caleb Rochelle did that to a girl. What a bully."

My mouth drops open in stunned surprise, and no words can even come out. Luckily, Linnie asks for me, "How did you know about that?"

Muriel grins at my daughter. "Well, you see, my daughter Rebecca is married to Silas Goddard's son, Silas Junior. Silas Senior was eavesdropping on Colt when he tore Caleb's daddy a new one. My understanding is Colt promised to visit on Jimmy tenfold whatever his son bestowed on you, darlin'. I guarantee you that boy won't be messing with you again."

I just continue to blink at Muriel, completely stunned she would know the circumstances of Colt's talk with that little bully's father just mere minutes after it happened.

I will never underestimate the power of the gossip mill again. It truly is better than CNN on delivering the most up-to-date news the fastest.

"You want a raw steak for that eye, honey?" Muriel asks.

"Huh?" Linnie says as her eyes grow wide behind her

glasses.

Muriel circles her finger in the air and then points directly at Linnie's black eye. "Raw steak. I've got a sirloin back there I'll give your mama for cost. Put it against that black eye, and it'll draw the bruise out faster than a whippoorwill's butt in mosquito season."

"Huh?" Linnie asks again.

I stifle a snicker and tell Muriel, "We're good. I put some ice on it already."

Muriel shakes her head. "Not as good as raw steak, but to each his own. Now, you girls know what you're going to have for dinner?"

I nod and order the meatloaf special for myself. Linnie orders a strawberry milkshake and fries. As Muriel turns away to put our order in, I see Floyd walking in the front door of the restaurant. He looks all around and when his eyes land on me and lock, he purposely starts heading our way, which means he came in here looking for us.

Floyd walks right up to our table. Without invitation or preamble, he pulls out one of the chairs and sets his bulky frame in it. Linnie has not had the pleasure of meeting Floyd yet, and she stares at him all agog.

Floyd puts his meaty arms on the table and leans toward my daughter. He studies her face for a moment and says, "I heard what happened. Colt handled it with Jimmy Rochelle just fine, but had he not, you rest assured I would've had your back, little girl."

Linnie just turns to look at me, and I can see a million questions in her gaze. I smile and jerk my chin toward Floyd. "This is Floyd. He owns the hardware store next door."

Linnie doesn't look at Floyd. It's almost as if she's terrified to take her gaze from mine and address the next eccentric character she's met here in the town of Whynot.

"He's a nice guy. He protects the town with a shotgun."

Linnie finally nods at me and turns a shy look toward Floyd. "I remember."

"Silas Goddard called me just now. He works out at Goddard Farms. Jimmy Rochelle was running his mouth about Colt coming out there. That's how I heard what happened."

This concerns me as Colt made it sound like everything was settled without any further issues. "Running his mouth? Do you think everything's okay?"

Floyd scratches at his scruffy beard and nods. "It's as right as rain, honey. Trust me, Jimmy Rochelle ain't stupid enough to tangle with Colt. He just likes to hear himself talk."

"So why do you protect the town with a shotgun if the town already has a police department?" Linnie asks Floyd, and he turns his gaze to her.

She seems to be completely over her discombobulation and is looking at him curiously. He smiles at her. At least I think it's a smile, but it's hard to tell under all that wiry gray beard that hangs down his chest. I do note his eyes crinkle a little at the corners.

"Well, that's a good question and one that I've been asked a lot. The short answer is… I love this town. Born and raised here. Never wanted to go anywhere else. I love all the people in it. And while I think we have a fine police force, they just can't patrol every inch of this town every night. So I lend my services to the good people of Whynot. Plus, I really like shooting my shotgun. Since it's illegal in the city limits, I feel extra important that they let me do that."

"They let you?" Linnie asks in awe.

Floyd shrugs. "I haven't been arrested yet."

"Can I patrol with you one night?" Linnie asks excitedly.

"Of course," Floyd says.

At the same exact time, I say, "Absolutely not."

Both ignore me and lapse into a conversation about town patrols and shotguns. My attention is redirected to the door that swings open, and I watch as Colt walks in.

Like Floyd, he lets his gaze roam around the restaurant until it locks with mine. His lips tip upward at the corners, and he saunters our way. My pulse goes bananas knowing this sweet, kind, and generous man just went and defended my daughter's honor by threatening to kick that little bully's dad's butt.

Now that is damn attractive.

As Colt pulls out the last chair at our table, Muriel calls out to him, "You want the special?"

"Yup," he calls back.

Muriel yells to Floyd. "What do you want?"

"I'll have the same. And bring me a sweet tea."

And just like that, we have two dinner companions and I couldn't be happier.

Colt is sitting to my right, and he leans toward me. His gaze cuts to Linnie briefly before settling back to me. "How is she?"

I give him a smile. "She's fine. We both are thanks to you handling that for us. Thank you again."

"It seriously was my pleasure, darlin'," Colt murmurs in a low voice that sends tingles up my spine. His voice drops an octave lower, and he leans in just a little closer so only I can hear, "Maybe you'll even give me a kiss one day in gratitude."

My voice is hoarse and raspy when I tell him, "I can probably accommodate that."

CHAPTER 18

Colt

"**G**LAD TO SEE you're back in action," I tell Pap as I take a sip of my draft beer. He's the best player on our dart team, and his absence while he recovered from surgery was deeply felt.

He steps up to the two-foot strip of silver duct tape that was pressed onto the scuffed wooden floor of Chesty's. It's placed at exactly seven feet, nine and a quarter inches from the board since we're playing steel-tipped.

I watch as he takes aim at the board. Pap has an unusual style. He holds his dart in front of him, not with the tip pointed at where's aiming but rather he holds it at an angle... as if he's holding a pen. Pap's gaze finds his target and his hand is steady.

With a mere flick of his wrist, the dart flies and hits exactly where he was aiming.

A trip twenty.

I grin, and the guys on the other team groan. Lowe records the sixty points on a chalkboard mounted on the wall near the throw line, and the twenties are closed for us. Cricket is our game of choice in this league.

"We should just forfeit if this is how Pap's shooting tonight," one of our opponents grumbles.

Pap lets loose his next dart. He almost hits a trip nineteen but only gets a single. This is rectified by his last dart, which hits the double nineteen, and just like that, our team has closed out two numbers and taken a huge lead.

While someone on the opposite team steps up to the line for their turn, Pap joins Lowe, Floyd, and me at a small square table that holds our beers. We're each sporting scarlet-colored t-shirts with the Chesty's logo on the back done in gold. The four of us have represented Chesty's in the Scuppernong county steel-tip dart league for six years now.

We've been reigning champions all six years.

From August through November, every Thursday night at seven, the four of us—with Trixie as an alternate in case one of us can't make it—meet at a hosting bar. Tonight, we play at Chesty's, but home field advantage isn't needed. Pap's the best player in the league, and it's sort of a cake walk for us.

"Jimmy Rochelle was in here the other night running his mouth about you," Pap says offhandedly. I pulled a chair over for him to sit in, but he's ignoring it.

Stubborn old man.

"Oh, yeah?" I ask with a smirk. "What did he say?"

"Just stuff that would make you want to go kick his butt right now, so I won't repeat it."

"He can talk crap all he wants," I tell Pap with confidence. "As long as he keeps his little hellion kid in check around Linnie."

"You're up, Colt," one of the other players call out.

Snatching my darts off the table, I step up to the line. I hold my dart tip pointed straight at my target. I tried Pap's method and it never works for me.

Trip seventeen… you're mine.

I pull my hand back, prepared to launch when Floyd says to me, "You told Darby you love her yet?"

My entire body jerks as my dart flies, not over Darby's

name, but from the word "love" that Floyd so casually tosses out. My dart veers left and sticks in the wood-paneled wall, causing the players on the other team to howl with laughter.

Turning, I see Pap and Lowe snickering at me, but Floyd merely looks at me expectantly for my answer.

"No," I growl with condescension. "I haven't told her I love her, Floyd."

Geez... how thick can Floyd actually be? I mean, I knew he had a few screws loose, but...

I turn back to face the dartboard and take aim at the trip seventeen again. This is my number, and I almost always get a triple.

Aim is taken and just before I let it loose, Floyd asks, "Well, why not? You shouldn't keep those things inside."

Once again, my dart sticks in the wall where it vibrates for a moment before going still.

The other team roars with laughter, and I turn a glare upon them. It doesn't have the intended effect, and they just laugh harder.

Spinning toward Floyd, I take three steps to come toe to toe with him. "Floyd. I don't love Darby so that's why I haven't told her. I've only known her a couple of weeks."

"Four and a half," he replies.

"Excuse me?"

"Four and a half weeks," Floyd clarifies. "You've known her four and a half weeks."

Yes, I know that's how long I've known her. I remember the exact day I met her in Laken's clinic. Why Floyd knows that date is both weird and right at the same time, but that's beside the point.

"I haven't even kissed her yet, Floyd." Talk about putting the cart before the horse.

"Which is plain stupid if you ask me," Floyd replies swiftly.

Lowe and Pap nod their heads in agreement, and I'm surprised neither throw their hands up and say something like, "Preach it, Floyd."

"A woman that looks like Darby," Pap intones because he's not going to ever sit quiet, "you should be kissing her."

"She's married," I mutter.

"Not for much longer," Floyd says knowingly, as if he's got the inside track into Darby's divorce proceedings. And knowing him, he probably does somehow. "Besides, she's been separated long enough to do some kissing. I'm beginning to wonder if you even like her at all."

"I like her," I blurt out to Floyd, disregarding Pap and Lowe's second round of snickers.

"Hey, Colt," one of the other players calls out. "Can you leave your hen party for just a few minutes and come shoot?"

I spin away from Floyd, Pap, and Lowe, and take three steps back to the line. I give quick aim, don't think too hard about any of it, and let my dart fly.

I'm turning my back on it just as soon as I see it stick the trip seventeen.

Walking back up to my hen party, because that's exactly what this has turned into, I lower my voice a bit. Lowe, Pap, and Floyd lean in to listen. "Look… I like Darby a lot. I mean, like more than anyone else I've dated. And that's just the thing… we haven't really dated. Dinner out once and I'm taking her and Linnie to the fair on Saturday, but that hardly makes for kissing circumstances."

"You're looking at it wrong," Floyd insists with a wag of his finger in my face. "She gave up a grant for you. You battled a bully for her daughter. You two are more than ready for some kissing."

"I'd get on it if I were you," Pap throws in.

Lowe nods. "Yup."

A long, low growl rumbles in my chest, and it's born of both frustration and an overwhelming sense of protectiveness for Darby. "She's not ready yet. I'm taking it slow because Darby needs to go slow."

"She told you this?" Floyd asks suspiciously.

"Well, no. But she was in a bad marriage for a very long time."

"Irrelevant," Floyd says and crosses his arms over his chest in defiance.

"It's not irrelevant," I snap at him.

It's so relevant. But it's also not seemingly holding Darby back, so why am I letting it hold me back?

Floyd, Pap, and Lowe just stare at me as if I've not said anything worth them uttering a response to. This ticks me off, so I point an index finger at them, going from left to right as it silently marks each. "None of you have any business giving me advice on women. Floyd... you've never been married or even had a girlfriend that I know of. You're married to your dang shotgun."

Floyd furrows his eyebrows, considering my words. I turn to Pap. "And you... you're too chicken to even ask Mary Margaret Quinn out for a date."

Pap flushes red and Lowe laughs, but his smile slides off his face when I turn to him. "And you—"

He holds up his hands in defense and smirks. "Hey... I'm in love and happily married."

I lean into him and taunt with an evil grin. "You got drunk in Vegas and married Mely in front of Elvis."

Lowe's jaw locks and his cheeks turn red with embarrassment.

"The point being," I say in a more conciliatory tone. "I know what I'm doing, okay? And slow is the name of the game."

Floyd opens his mouth, no doubt to argue I should move faster, but the door to the bar flies open and we all turn to look.

A tall, black man with a bald head walks in followed by Mely. He's outrageously dressed in a pair of aqua-colored skinny jeans with matching suede loafers on his feet. A shiny silver shirt sparkles from the neon beer lights all around. He throws his arms up over his head. In a loud voice, he announces, "Morri D has arrived."

Mely's best friend comes down to visit us often from New York and has officially been adopted by Whynot as sort of our official mascot that shows we're a progressive and accepting southern town.

Well, most of us anyway. There are a few who look down their noses at him, but not here in Chesty's. Pap's made it perfectly clear it won't be tolerated in here.

"Pap," Morri yells as his eyes light on my grandfather.

The two men hug, then Morri's kissing Lowe once on each cheek, a feat that has Pap, Floyd, and me now howling with laughter as Lowe tries to dodge Morri's lips.

I notice Mely comes to stand quietly beside me, just watching Morri and his antics with a soft smile on her face. She speaks from the side of her mouth to me, "Is it bad I love the way Morri loves to torture Lowe?"

"Not at all," I assure her.

Morri gives a hug to Floyd next, whereby it's no surprise Floyd gives it back tenfold. He wraps Morri in a huge bear hug, lifts him off his feet, and spins him around. This may seem at odds with the big, gruff mountain of a redneck man who patrols town with a shotgun, but Floyd and Morri have become good friends over the last few months when Morri visits us. In fact, Morri took Floyd to a drag show on one of his visits.

Morri is only slightly more reserved with me when he turns my way. I don't even bother to try to hold my hand out for a handshake, knowing it would be ignored and I'd probably get kisses on my cheeks, too. Instead, I decide to open my arms up and accept a warm hug from him, although I punctuate my affection with some manly claps on his back.

He doesn't fully release me, rather keeping his hands on my shoulders. He looks deeply into my eyes for a moment. Then his chin tucks in and he coos, "Oh, baby... you got it bad, don't you?"

"What?" I ask, completely perplexed.

"Love. You've been hit by the love bug. I can see it in your eyes. In the set to your shoulders. Hell, I can smell it coming off you. Plus... Floyd texted me and told me all about your pretty peach farmer."

Lowe, Pap, Floyd, Mely, and the entire opposing dart team howl with laughter. Morri doesn't crack a smile but just nods. "Mmm. Hmmm. Totally bit by the bug."

I pull out of Morri's grasp and roll my eyes. It's enough of a denial, but the one thing I would admit to if he asked me right now is I do feel something strong for Darby, and I bet it only gets stronger.

CHAPTER 19

Darby

EVEN AT THIRTY-ONE, raising a child for seven years, almost completing a PhD, and weathering a bad marriage, I'm still lacking the confidence to pull the door open without doing a final check of myself.

I unnecessarily smooth my hair I'd put into a ponytail, check my attire choice for the hundredth time, and put my hand in front of my mouth to puff some air out so I can check that my breath still smells minty after the vigorous brushing I gave them a few minutes ago. Satisfied, I open my front door and greet Colt with a smile.

Gosh, he looks good. Wearing nothing fancy—because why would he? We're going to the state fair. But he makes it look like jeans were God-made just to fit his body and for no other reason at all. He's got on an olive-green Henley and a dark blue windbreaker because it's a little nippy outside. It's going to heat up later today, so I also decided on layers for both Linnie and me.

And here Colt stands on my porch, ready to take me out on a date. And yes, even though he's taking both Linnie and me to the fair, there's no doubt this is a date. It could be confusing to some because after our first dinner date, we've not made plans yet for another one on one. One could even say the mere fact he specifically chose to do something with Linnie keeps this strictly in the friend zone.

But I know differently. I knew for sure he wasn't interested in the friend zone when he asked point blank if I'd give him a kiss at some point as a thank you for handling Linnie's bully. It wasn't just the words that spoke volumes, but the tone of his voice and the message in his eyes was clear.

He's interested in me in a romantic nature, and God help me... I'm interested right back. I hadn't planned this, but I also can't ignore something—someone—who feels just so very right.

"Gonna invite me in?" Colt asks lightly with eyebrows raised.

I startle and push the screen door open so fast he has to take a quick step back so I don't pop him in the face. That causes me to laugh almost hysterically, and Colt's also chuckling as he steps inside.

He gives me a once over as I shut the door behind him. Not lewdly nor overtly, but in a subtly appreciative way. I'm not wearing anything special at all—jeans and a lightweight sweater—but I know he likes it when he says, "You look tremendously pretty today, Darby."

I can feel the blush all the way through to the roots of my hair, but I let my flirt work. "You're looking mighty fine, too, Colt."

We just stare at each other, almost as if we're both stuck in a trance. It would be a good time to have our first kiss, but it would also be fine to wait. We just stare at each other, the silence in no way awkward, until Linnie yells down from her bedroom. "M-o-o-o-m-m-m...where are my white hairbows?"

Colt jumps straight up as Linnie sometimes has no volume control when she calls out to me. I merely jerk in place, give Colt an apologetic smile, and call back up to her not quite so loudly, "I'm not sure, honey. Last I saw them they were on your dresser."

"I need them," she laments… loudly.

"Then I suggest you look harder," I return.

Colt chuckles at our exchange, and I smile back at him. In a much quieter voice, I add on to him alone, "Joys of a seven-year-old girl."

"Because the color of your hairbows is important," Colt replies solemnly.

"That they are," I agree, and turn toward the kitchen that sits just beyond the staircase. "I was just finishing up the breakfast dishes. Would you like something to drink? She'll be down in a few minutes."

"I'm good," he says as he follows me into the kitchen. "Besides… I'm a few minutes early."

A knock on the door startles me again, but then I consider it's probably just Carlos needing something. I wave a hand toward the small dinette table. "Make yourself at home. I'll be right back."

I make my way to the front door. When I pull it open, I see Mitch standing on the other side of the screen door. Anger heats me up from the inside out as I step up to the screen, but I make no move to open it. How dare he just show up again unannounced and expect he's going to take Linnie to go sit in a hotel room while he works for the weekend?

"What are you doing here?" I ask, trying to keep my tone level and non-accusing.

He answers by opening the screen door and walking right inside. I think for a moment about blocking him and insisting he stay out on the porch, but that will just raise his ire. He brushes past me. In an effort to rein him in, so he doesn't wander too far into my house, I ask again, "What are you doing here, Mitch?"

He turns to face me, his voice clipped. "I came to see my daughter. Is that a crime?"

"It's not a crime, but it's certainly rude to show up out of the blue and expect she'll just be sitting here with nothing to do. As it is, we have plans."

"Well, that's fine, but I still want to see Linnie for a little bit. I have really exciting news for her." The tone of his voice comes across as ominous. I know with certainty that whatever news he has, it's not going to set well with me.

"And what would that be?" I ask quietly.

"I'm going to be working from the Raleigh office for the foreseeable future. I'm going to do a short-term lease on an apartment."

"What does the foreseeable future mean?" My throat is gritty, and my palms start to sweat.

He shrugs, his smile almost leering. "Long enough to establish domicile here. Looks like the North Carolina courts will be governing the divorce proceedings."

I suck in a deep breath through my nose, keeping my lips clamped shut tightly so I don't scream out at him in frustration. I'm not stupid. I know what this means as my attorney had made a passing comment to me the other day when I'd given him the free rein to go after Mitch hard.

He'd said, "Be glad you're not filing in North Carolina, Darby. You have to wait a year from the date you separate in order to get divorced."

There's not a doubt in my mind Mitch is doing this to stall the proceedings. He's moved here to not only get residence, but to possibly keep pushing at me to reconcile—which will never happen.

"Now, if you don't mind," Mitch continues smoothly. "I'd like to see Linnie so I can tell her the good news. I'm sure your plans can wait just a few minutes."

It's at this moment that Colt meanders out of the kitchen. At first, I'm not sure if he could hear what was going on in here or if he just unexpectedly walked into a heated discussion between two adversaries. But when he walks up behind Mitch and looks at me over his shoulder, I can tell by his eyes he walked in here on purpose in case things got out of hand. He must have heard what was going on.

Mitch hears Colt's footsteps and spins toward him. I'm standing at enough of an angle from Mitch that I can see the side of his face, and his eyes go winter cold as he takes in the man standing in his wife's house. The muscle at the corner of his jaw starts jumping, and a red flush creeps up the back of his neck.

"Who the hell are you?" Mitch demands.

Colt gives him a lazy smile and leans against the edge of the staircase bannister, crossing his arms casually over his chest. "A friend of Darby's."

Mitch scoffs and then sneers at Colt. "Friends? Yeah, right."

Colt's demeanor doesn't change. He just smiles pleasantly at Mitch, who then turns his fury my way. Spinning back to me, he practically hisses. "You're a married woman, for God's sake, Darby. And here you are with another man in your house?"

I could laugh over the irony, coming from a man who has had a mistress for a very long time. But because I don't care about that, or any of Mitch's thoughts to be honest, I simply say, "Colt is a friend but even if he was more, it's none of your business. We are legally separated and whether I pursue a divorce in Illinois or North Carolina, it's going to happen."

Mitch's face mottles red with fury and veins pop out on

his temple. I've seen him this angry a time or two, and I can't help but flinch in anticipation over the nasty, vile things I know he's getting ready to unleash. I even have a moment of pre-embarrassment that Colt is going to see this.

Shaking his finger at me, Mitch lets loose with his venom. "You are and always were an incompetent wife. Never understanding your place. A complete failure at everything, even raising our daughter."

I don't take my eyes off Mitch, but I can see Colt from my peripheral vision push off the wall and his posture become rigid.

"You're going to regret this, Darby," Mitch continues without pause or barely taking a breath. "For all the trouble and misery you've caused and are continuing to cause, you're going to regret not taking the easy out I've offered you."

I can't help but retort. "And what's that, Mitch? Coming back to you? Because there would be nothing easy about that. In fact, it's not a choice at all."

"You'll regret saying that, too," he snarls at me menacingly, and I take a step backward. Colt takes a step toward Mitch, but I give a tiny shake of my head.

He doesn't heed me and speaks rather than acts. "I think it's time you left," he says to Mitch in a low voice. "Before this gets out of control."

Mitch whirls on Colt and yells. "You don't tell me what to do, you country bumpkin."

Some might find this brave since Colt has several inches on Mitch and over a decade of youth, but Mitch has too big of an ego to ever be intimidated. He would never think in a million years that his mouth could get him in physical trouble—like the kind that ends with Colt's fist on Mitch's jaw.

I step forward and put my hand on Mitch's arm, hoping to restrain him by a simple soft touch of caution. But he's so angry and out of control that he flings me off with a violent swing of his arm toward me. He wasn't trying to hit me, but only by my quick reflexes and scuttling backward was it prevented.

It seems to happen in slow motion, but Colt starts for Mitch. Everything is spiraling out of control, and I have a moment's hesitation on whether I should jump in between them.

Then Linnie's voice cuts through the haze of indecision. She yells from the top of the staircase, "You leave my mommy alone."

Everyone freezes, and Mitch turns to look up at his daughter. She's got tears in her eyes and true to habit, she pushes her glasses up her nose. Her arms then drop, her little hands balling into tight fists of aggression. "You leave her and me alone. I don't want to see you."

"Linnie, honey," I say imploringly to her, not to give her father a chance but for her to just look at me and give me some indication she's not being scarred for life.

To my consternation, she spins and runs back to her room, slamming the door behind her.

For a moment, I feel dizzy. Although I've never in my life passed out or fainted, I kind of wish for the oblivion. But that escape is not for me.

Colt steps toward Mitch, and his voice is so hard and unyielding I snap to attention. He leans in to my hopefully soon-to-be ex-husband. With no need to speak above a murmur, he says, "You can leave on your own two feet out that front door, or I can help you along a little quicker. Your welcome here has officially been worn out."

Mitch glares at Colt—or rather, up at Colt—and seems to understand suddenly that he could easily go flying out the front door.

Of course, he has to have the last word. His eyes snap to mine, and he points a threatening finger at me. "Big mistake here today, Darby. Big mistake."

I swallow hard, but don't let my gaze upon him falter. I manage to lift my chin in defiance, but I know the first thing on my agenda come Monday morning is to find a very good and aggressive North Carolina lawyer to help me out.

Mitch stomps out of the house, slamming the door behind him. I watch it for a few moments before turning shamefaced to Colt. "I'm so sorry you had to witness that."

Colt walks up to me, his face awash with empathy. He brings a hand to my shoulder where it slides to the back of my neck. He leans down, putting his face before mine. "Don't you dare apologize for that jackass."

I shake my head despite his hold on me. "My life is a mess, Colt. You should walk away."

"Don't want to," he says stubbornly, his eyes never wavering from mine. "But I am going to call off our trip to the fair right now. Linnie's upset, and I think you need to go talk to her. Get her settled down."

"She has to be scared Mitch is here to take her away or something," I agree with a nod. I give a tremulous smile. "Again… I'm really sorry, Colt. That was just plain embarrassing."

"Your soon-to-be ex is a real jerk," he mutters. "But there's light at the end of the tunnel. You'll be rid of him one day."

I nod again, and then to my surprise, Colt leans into me. Not to kiss me on the lips, but to press his forehead to mine in a soft gesture of support. He squeezes my neck once and then turns for the door.

When he reaches it, he tells me, "I'm going over to talk to Jake. I guarantee you he has contacts and can get to work on finding you a good attorney here in North Carolina."

I ordinarily would push back at such help, not only for Colt stepping in but now Jake getting involved once more into my mess. But the truth is Mitch just rattled me. While he's always been a bully and verbal abuser, I saw something in his eyes I hadn't really seen before.

A sort of deranged anger that didn't look like it could be quenched by anything short of my absolute submission to him. And because that's not going to happen, I'm not sure what lengths Mitch is going to go to make my life hard.

CHAPTER 20

Colt

"**E**VERYTHING LOOKS REALLY good," Lowe says as we walk down a row of freshly planted vitis rotundfolia, or muscadine grapes. In particular, I planted the Ison muscadine which is relatively new to the wine-making industry. I chose it because it gives greater yield. For a fledgling winery wanting to get quickly established, this was a good risk to take.

"Agreed," I say. I reach out to touch one of the vines that will be trained to grow up the trellises we built. I'd taken to coming out here each morning to check on things. It's unnecessary and overprotective, but it's also my family's future.

I decided to eat breakfast with Mama and Dad this morning, driving the Gator over to their house from my cabin. I found Lowe and Mely digging into biscuits and gravy, and Dad grumbling over an egg-white omelet because his cholesterol is too high. When I headed out to check on my newly established vineyard, Lowe hopped in the Gator and rode out with me.

This was unsurprising. Lowe may be a carpenter by trade, but farming is still in his blood. Out of all of us Mancinkus kids, heritage and tradition are the most important to him. That is totally evidenced by the fact he once boarded up all the windows and doors of Mainer House after Mely had bought it and defended the place with a gun even though our family didn't own it anymore.

But heck… that turned out well for them as they're married now.

Lowe asked a dozen different questions about wine making on the short ride over, holding onto the outside frame as we bounce along the rutted dirt road. He continues to ask them.

"What kind of facility are you going to build for the actual wine making?" he asks me.

I point to the western ridge of the property. "Over there. We're going to have to clear some trees, of course. Bring in some fill dirt."

"What size building do you need?"

"Maybe six or seven thousand square feet," I tell him. It's all laid out in my business plan, but Lowe hasn't read it. He won't, either. He'll trust I know what I'm doing even if I'm learning a lot of this as I go along.

"I'll handle it," he says firmly, and this is also not a surprise.

My brother can build anything. He built the cabin I'm now living in as his first home, and he did it all on his own outside of having a few buddies helping him with the framing. I personally helped him lay the drywall and a few other things that required two sets of hands. But for the most part, every nail and shingle on that place was done by Lowe.

"I figure we'll need to build at the end of year two, but we can really get started anytime since we got all the time in the world."

Lowe nods. "Sooner, I say. That will let me tinker with something when Mely's busy."

"Busy doing what?" I ask curiously.

His wife is an interior designer and flips houses by trade,

but she was going to cut the business way back, so she didn't have to travel as much. She's talented, highly sought out, and has clients all over the United States and even abroad.

Lowe shrugs and doesn't answer me right away, and that hesitation means he's hiding something. That just won't do. "What, dude? What do you mean by Mely being busy?"

He still says nothing, but reaches above to test the strength of one of the load-bearing wires on a trellis.

My eyes round as a thought strikes me. "She's pregnant, isn't she?"

I thought she'd eaten a lot at breakfast.

But that's not it as Lowe's head snaps my way and gives me a look like I'm stark raving mad. "God no, she's not pregnant. We just got married."

"So," I say with careless shrug. "People get pregnant all the time."

Lowe just takes a couple of steps my way and lowers his voice so we can't be heard, which is moot given we're in the middle of a vineyard with no one around. "Mely made an offer on Millie's about a month ago."

I nod my head. That wasn't a secret, and I think Larkin told me about it. "And?"

"And they accepted it," Lowe says in a hushed tone. "And now it looks like we're the proud owners of Millie's Bed and Breakfast."

"Why are you whispering?" I ask him.

"Because we haven't told anyone yet," he says with a roll of her eyes. "Mely wants to announce it to the family when we're all together at the wedding Friday, so you better act damn surprised when she drops the bomb, you hear me?"

"I hear you," I say with a chuckle as I clap him on the shoulder. "But that's awesome news, brother. Does that mean she'll give up the design business?"

"Yeah," Lowe says with a soft smile forming on his face. "She'll be here all the time now."

I just stare at my brother while his eyes sort of gloss over with happiness and he looks dopey as all get out, but I love seeing him like this. We're dudes, and we don't really talk about dreams and aspirations about finding love, but when he did, it sure as hell made me happy for him.

I snap my fingers in front of his eyes. He blinks before giving me a sheepish grin. "Sorry."

"You're pathetic." I try to put some condescension in my voice, but it totally fails because Lowe laughs.

"You're just jealous," he says with a jab to my shoulder with his fist. I'm bigger than Lowe so it doesn't even rock me. "But hey... I should have asked. How was your 'date' yesterday with Darby at the fair?"

And when he said 'date,' he made air quotes with his fingers. I'd filled him in Thursday night while playing darts about my plans to take Darby and Linnie to the fair, and thus ensued a long argument over if it was really a date since Linnie was coming along. I insisted it was not, but every other person in Chesty's that Lowe asked for an opinion insisted it was.

He literally asked every person in there, stating he was doing an informal poll.

"We didn't go." My glum tone has his smile sliding right off his face and worry replacing it.

"What happened?"

"Her husband happened," I mutter as I head back toward the Gator. Lowe follows silently behind me, but I know he wants and expects more details. "Showed up at her house just as we were getting ready to leave. Made a real ass of himself and got Linnie all upset. So we cancelled, but maybe we can go next weekend."

"You don't sound so enthused about it," Lowe muses as we climb into the Gator.

"Just not sure if this is workable," I tell him as I head back down the road that will take us to the main farmhouse.

"Surely you're not going to let some jackass stand in your way—"

I cut Lowe off, so he doesn't misunderstand me further. "I won't let it stand in my way, but I can see Darby letting it. She was really embarrassed about how he acted, and Lowe—this guy is a class-A jerk. He was talking about how Darby didn't understand her place. It was like he stepped out of the fifties or something."

"How did you not take a swing at him?" Lowe asks sort of serious but sort of joking.

"I about did," I admit. "But Linnie was there, and I didn't want things to escalate."

"So what's standing in the way if you're not going to back down?" he asks.

"Darby will stand in the way of herself," I reply. I drive past the front of the farmhouse and to the small detached garage where we keep the Gator. I don't pull it in as I'll be back on it later to do some fence repairs around the cattle pastures. "She told me I should walk away from her. She might just use him as an excuse to push me away."

"So don't let her," he says simply as we get out of the vehicle.

When I look over at him, he nods at something behind me. I turn to see Darby's BMW coming down the road. She still hasn't gotten a farm truck, and I told her I'd help her look for one when she was ready.

Lowe comes around and claps his hand on my shoulder.

Giving it a squeeze, he says, "Get her, tiger."

My stomach rolls slightly even as I nod at my brother with confidence. If Darby is here to break things off, I'm prepared to talk her out of it.

I walk to the edge of the driveway. After she brings her car to a stop, I lean over to open the driver's door for her. "Fancy meeting you here," I quip.

She grins and extends her legs out of the car, gracefully exiting. I shut the door for her. "Hope I'm not intruding."

"No at all," I tell her. "Just finished breakfast and drove out to check out the vines with Lowe. Want something to eat?"

She shakes her head. "No, thank you. Linnie and I had waffles this morning."

"How is she?" I ask, my voice lowering to a grave tone as I cross my arms over my chest.

"She's fine," Darby says with a brave smile, but I can tell by the haunted look in her eyes that although Linnie may be fine this morning, she wasn't last night. Not after what happened.

"Does she understand that wasn't about her?" I've never heard Darby utter a negative thing about Linnie's dad in front of her, but the same can't be said about what Mitch said last night.

Darby gives a wry laugh and tucks her hair behind one ear. "I wish it was more about Linnie, sometimes. I mean… that he'd show genuine interest in her, but as you could see… it's not like that with him."

"He's definitely got an obsession for you," I acknowledge, letting my arms drop away from my chest.

"He's not going to go away quietly," she whispers as she looks up at me. "It's going to be a bitter battle. I wanted to come out here and tell you... maybe you should just move on from me."

"Yeah," I drawl out as if I'm considering her words. I shake my head. "Not going to work for me. I don't want to move on."

To my surprise, because I expected a bit of a fight, Darby lets out a relieved laugh. "Good. Because I don't want you to move on either."

"Then why did you drive out here to tell me to take a hike?" I tease. I take a step in closer to her, unable to control my own laugh.

Her laughter ceases, but her smile stays in place. "I wanted to give you one last chance to run. But I won't do that again."

"That works out nicely for me then," I say as I step even closer to her. I bring a hand to her hip, the other to the side of her face. Her eyes are so clear and trusting as she blinks up at me. "I think I'm going to have that first kiss right now."

"That would be an awesome idea," she murmurs.

It doesn't matter we're in broad daylight in front of my parents' house, or that we didn't just finish a romantic date that would end perfectly with our first kiss.

No, this is absolutely the right time.

My lips touch hers, and I'm almost bowled over by the surge of adrenaline that floods my entire body. Darby feels it too because she gasps. We pull back, both of us wide eyed and staring at each other.

"That was—"

"Wow."

"Just... wow."

I kiss her again, and it's so "wow". Both my hands come to her face as I tilt my head and deepen the kiss. My tongue touches hers gently, and she makes a kitteny purr deep in her throat.

With my heart pounding and about to burst out of my chest, I reluctantly pull back from her mouth. There's no doubt in my mind it could ignite into something that would be uncontrollable, and *now* is definitely not the time for *that*.

"So, um… that was… nice," she says, her cheeks pink and her expression bordering on flustered.

I give a tiny cough to clear my throat, which is dry as the desert right now. "Yeah… nice."

We stare at each other a moment, then both of us burst out laughing. I reach out and snag her by the shoulders, pulling her into me. She presses a hand, then a cheek, to my chest, and I wrap my arms around her back, giving her a hug.

"It was more than nice," I murmur. "And I can't wait to see how much nicer it will get in time."

"Agreed," she says softly.

"Few things we need to get straight," I tell her, and she pulls back to look up at me curiously. "First, what days this week can you get away from the farm to meet me for lunch?"

Her eyes twinkle. "Any day."

"Good answer," I say thoughtfully. "And Friday night is Della and Jason's wedding party. I'd like to take you and Linnie. It's going to be a lot of fun, and Della told me to invite you."

Darby smiles softly. "Okay… we're in."

"And finally," I say dramatically. "We're doing the fair on Sunday. Nothing is going to ruin those plans, not even Mitch. Got it?"

"Got it," she says. By the tone of her voice, you'd think I'd just lassoed the moon for her. The resulting swell of satisfaction within me is something I've never quite felt before. It makes me want to beat on my chest and howl for some reason.

CHAPTER 21

Darby

A LL WEDDINGS SHOULD be done this way. I've never seen such a fun, joyous atmosphere that is both magical and laid-back at the same time. Della and Jason chose to do a very short, simple civil ceremony and rented out the old train depot that sits on the eastern side of Whynot for a huge party after.

Although trains still rumble through town carrying God knows what freight, Colt told me the depot hasn't been open for as long as he can remember. I guess once upon a time, passenger trains would stop here but not any longer. It has since been renovated and is nothing more than a long, rectangular hall that people can use for weddings or any other type of party or function.

Jason and Della chose to get married in jeans and cowboy boots. Jason chose a white Western-style shirt while Della went with a more flowing white gauzy blouse. She has autumn-colored flowers ringed around her head in orange, yellow, and red. All the tables are decorated with mums and fall leaves and they hired a band to play rock 'n roll from the seventies.

Mostly to my delight is the food. I get to experience a true Eastern North Carolina pig picking complete with chopped and pulled pork, coleslaw, and hushpuppies. I've eaten so much I swear I probably gained ten pounds tonight.

Larkin outdid herself on the cake. She didn't do anything fancy, and Della hadn't wanted the little plastic bride and groom on the top. Instead, they decided to go with just big fat roses done in white buttercream frosting all over the three-layered cake. Because there are so many guests, Larkin did matching cupcakes and there are six dozen of them surrounding the main cake on the table.

Best of all, Linnie is having a wonderful time. There are some kids from her school here as well as some kids she has just met, and they are all running around like they don't have a care in the world. Linnie definitely seems to be gaining more confidence in this new life we've established here. Hopefully the way she's making new friends will help erase the bad memories of bullies such as Caleb Rochelle.

Linnie and I have been welcomed into and absorbed by the large Mainer-Mancinkus clan. We commandeered two large round tables near each other and pulled them together. The entire family is here including those who have recently been drawn in by love or marriage.

I'm, of course, the exception to that rule since it's neither love nor marriage that has me sitting here right now, but it definitely is something.

I definitely *have* something with Colt Mancinkus, although I have no clue where this is going. I find myself not overly bothered by this fact. I have no expectations, and I know enough about Colt to accept he's not toying with me. But whatever this is, it's so fresh and exciting and unlike anything I've ever experienced that I don't want it to ever end.

I think Colt may be perhaps the finest man I've ever had the pleasure of knowing outside of my own father.

I'm sitting next to Colt, having turned the chairs around to face the band, and I'm tapping my foot to Lynard Skynyrd.

My parents used to listen to this music a lot.

A man steps into my line of sight, and I blink as I look up at him. He's average height with nondescript brown hair and even more nondescript brown eyes. He looks at Colt, who nods at him in greeting before turning to me. He extends a hand out. "Darby, my name is Billy Crump."

I shake his hand and smile up at him. "It's a pleasure to meet you. Is that the same Crump as Crump's grocery store?"

He nods. "My daddy owns it, and I guess I'll own it one day. I run the butcher counter over there so if you ever need anything, you just give me a call."

We release hands, and I say, "That's very nice of you."

Billy glances left and then right as if he's expecting someone to overhear our conversation, which would be nearly impossible with the band playing music not too far away. As it stands, he's had to raise his voice a few decibels to make the introduction.

But he squats down in front of me and leans in a little closer. I look over to Colt, who's smirking at us before turning back to Billy.

"I'm sure you don't know this because why would you, but you see... I have a little side business. It ain't exactly legal, but it is profitable."

I just blink in confusion as I stare at Billy.

He continues. "I make peach moonshine. Everyone around here drinks it, including Chief Sumwalt of the police department. I make all kinds of moonshine actually, but the peach is my specialty and I heard you were starting a peach orchard. I thought perhaps you and I could come to some type of arrangement whereby you provide me peaches and I would pay you in kind with some moonshine."

I continue to just blink at Billy Crump as his proposition

is unlike anything that's ever been offered to me before. I can't even open my mouth to form words to come out because I wouldn't even know what to say to him.

Colt saves the day when he leans over and claps Billy on the shoulder. "Darby will take your offer into consideration, but she's probably going to be selling wholesale to major buyers, Billy."

"Oh yeah… right," Billy says, nodding his head vigorously. He then winks down at me. "But if you got a few extra peaches laying around, I'd be glad to take them off your hands."

I can't help but laugh. "You got it."

Billy meanders off, and Colt scoots his chair in closer to me. He loops an arm casually over the back of my chair and lets his fingers trail along my upper arm. So far, this is the closest Colt has gotten to me all evening, and I know this is in deference to Linnie. We had talked about it some at lunch this week—how we could continue to get to know each other and make it comfortable for Linnie as well.

The band finishes a song. Before they start the next, the lead singer puts his mouth up to the microphone. "Come on, Colt. Get your butt up here and do a song with us."

Several people in the crowd whistle and others chant Colt's name. The man beside me grins and shakes his head, making a dismissive wave of his hand at the band.

"Come on, Colt," the lead singer cajoles into the microphone. "Bet that pretty girl next to you would like to hear you sing."

"I really would," I add, and Colt's hazel eyes come to mine.

"If that's the case, I guess I need to go sing," is all he says as he pushes from his chair.

He's going to sing because I asked him to. Thank God I'm sitting down, or I would be in danger of swooning.

Everyone whistles louder as Colt saunters up to the make-shift stage and hops up on it. I look around at everyone clapping, and still others stopping conversations to watch Colt. It's clear he's beloved in this community, and I'm betting not just because of his singing voice.

The lead singer hands over his guitar to Colt, who puts it on as if he was born to wear it. He tests a few strings and then says something to the band.

"Wish he wouldn't have quit that band," Larkin says with a huff as she sits down in Colt's abandoned chair.

I blink in surprise. "Colt played in that band?"

She nods with a smile. "For several years. It was nothing major. You know, they do weddings and stuff, but at least it let Colt pursue his love of music somewhat."

"Why did he quit?" I ask.

"He just got busier with the farm. Didn't have time to practice and soon after, he didn't have time to do events."

I look back up at Colt, who looks so natural standing up there—as well as sexy as all get out—and it makes me sad all the things he's sacrificed for his farm and his family. It's just another reason why I like him so much.

To my surprise, the music starts as a slow ballad, which is a startling contrast to the upbeat rock music that's been playing. I recognize it immediately as an old George Strait song, *I Cross My Heart*.

And oh, wow... can he sing some country music. He sounds even better doing the classics. His eyes sweep out over the crowd, many stepping onto the dance floor to take advantage of a beautiful love song. Jason and Della take the center, and everyone watches them for a few moments before they start dancing themselves.

Occasionally, Colt's eyes come to me and he smiles as he sings. I feel the heat in my face and the mad thump of my heart. It would be beyond romantic to be dancing to this song with Colt, but just listening to him croon about dreams and promises is almost too much to bear.

As we look into the future.
It's as far as we can see.

Our eyes lock, and he doesn't look away for the rest of the song. My skin prickles as I realize he's making a very public proclamation that he's interested in me. I would guess by the way I'm staring back at him, I'm doing the same.

The song winds down… ends with Colt belting out the last deep note so it practically vibrates in my bones. Everyone goes crazy, cheering, whistling, and stamping their feet. Colt gives a dismissive wave of his hand, and says into the microphone, "Thank you."

After he removes the guitar, he hands it back to the lead singer, who says they're going to take a fifteen-minute break. He hops off the stage and walks with a natural swagger that's not put on, but every bit earned by his charisma and confidence.

"That was unbelievable," I tell him as he approaches. I stand just as he reaches me, and it would be the perfect moment to kiss.

You know, if the entire Mancinkus clan weren't sitting at the table watching and my seven-year-old daughter wasn't playing with the other kids fifteen feet away.

"Glad you liked it," he says as he chucks me under the chin with his fingers.

"Okay, I've got an announcement to make everyone," Mely says from the opposite side of the table. Colt, Larkin, and I both turn that way. The rest of the family is all present with empty plates of food and drink glasses in front of them.

Mely stands up and places her fingertips on the edge of the table. Lowe reaches a hand up from where he sits beside her to give her butt a little pat of encouragement. She grins at him.

When she looks back, she gives a little cough to clear her throat and says without any fanfare, "You're looking at the proud new owner of Millie's B&B."

Lowe gives a coughing sound. "Ahem."

Mely laughs and adds, "I mean owners. As in plural. Lowe and I bought it, and we're going to be opening it next month."

For a brutally painful moment, there's utter silence around the table. My heart hurts for Mely and Lowe that they're not getting family support, but then a dull roar rises as everyone starts exclaiming in excited surprise at once.

"Oh, my God," Larkin says as she runs around the table to practically tackle Mely in a hug. "I'm so thrilled."

After that, the family members—original and newly added—all swarm around Mely and Lowe for hugs and back claps of congratulations. I move my way around the table to do the same, content to wait my turn. Just as Colt steps up to his brother, Pap sidles in beside me. He puts his arm around my shoulder and gives me a squeeze.

"Does my heart good," he says as we watch Colt talking to Mely and Lowe.

"Seeing your brood succeed?" I hazard a guess.

"Well, that," he replies agreeably, but then turns his gaze to me. "But I enjoy seeing this community grow from the outside in. First Ry from Boston, then Mely from New York, and finally Jake from Chicago… all finding a new home here in Whynot. Just like I did all those years ago."

"It's a lovely sentiment," I tell Pap.

"You stick around here, and that would be another fine addition to our community," he points out.

Sly old dog. I know where you're going with this.

"That's sweet of you to say," I reply noncommittally, not because I'm unwilling to consider a permanent move here. On the contrary, this would be an amazing place to raise Linnie, but I don't engage in "what-ifs" with Pap because this thing with Colt is newly forming and I don't want to jinx it.

Pap grunts in frustration that I won't give him any clue as to my thoughts, but I just give him a polite smile back. Then I step up beside Colt and join him in congratulating his brother and sister-in-law.

CHAPTER 22

Colt

"**W**ATCH IT," LOWE calls. "You're going to hit the doorjamb."

I growl at my brother as Jake and I carefully, and without any error, maneuver a loveseat into the sitting room of Millie's. "You're awfully bossy for someone who doesn't seem to be doing any of the actual physical work."

"I've got ice-cold beer for the two of you," Lowe points out as if that excuses his overbearing manners.

I just grunt in acknowledgment as Jake and I carry the loveseat to place in front of the window as Lowe had imperiously directed.

We set it down and turn to look at my brother expectantly for our next assignment. So far, we have carried in two high-backed chairs, a coffee table, a sideboard, and a dining room table that seats eight. In fairness to Lowe, he helped bring in the dining room chairs.

"Where did Mely get all this furniture?" Jake asks.

When I arrived this morning to help Lowe move furniture per his request, I was stunned to find a large moving truck in front of Millie's blocking a good chunk of the road.

"She had me drive up to High Point a few days ago, and we picked all of this out. It was a lot cheaper for us to just bring it back ourselves in a rented U-Haul."

"Because you had free muscle labor," I mutter.

"Exactly," Lowe says with a huge grin. "Besides, I know you're going to have my butt out there harvesting grapes at some point."

"And don't forget you promised to build the actual winery portion," I remind him.

"You two definitely have a quid-pro-quo deal worked out," Jake says, butting into the conversation. "But what do I get in return for this?"

Lowe nods toward a cooler sitting in the foyer. "Like I said... I brought beer. And Colt and I won't harass you for dating our sister."

"A beer sounds like a good idea," I say as I head that way. "Let's have one now."

"But we have to unload the bedroom furniture," Lowe replies, following Jake and me out of the sitting room.

Bending over, I open the cooler Lowe had waiting in the foyer, pulling three beers out. I hand one to Jake and one to Lowe, then twist the cap off mine. I take a long swallow before I finally reply to my brother. "And I think we need a break before we do the upstairs furniture."

"It's hot as Hades in here," Jake says as he opens the front door. "Let's sit out on the front porch."

Millie's Bed and Breakfast has been an establishment in Whynot, North Carolina for decades. After Millie died, her sons let it run into the ground until it was unfortunately closed. It was the only place for lodging in our town. While the inside was a complete mess and Lowe had been hired by a real estate development company that bought it in foreclosure, the outside bones were still good.

It's a Victorian-style house with a wide sweeping porch that ends in rounded turrets on both sides. They go up two stories, ending in a conical roof with a spire and gray decorative shingles.

The clapboard siding is done in a buttercup yellow and the trim in bright white. Black shutters adorn every window, and Mely has put out several rocking chairs so people can sit out front and stare across the street at the beautiful courthouse.

Jake and I take two of the rocking chairs while Lowe leans back against the porch banister facing us. He crosses one leg over the other and takes a sip of his beer. "You got most of your stuff moved down here?"

That question is directed at Jake, who nods in affirmation. "Yeah… for the most part. I'm going to have to put some of it in storage up there when I put my apartment up for sale."

"I thought you were going to keep it since you're going to be working some out of your Chicago office?" I ask.

He shakes his head. "I'm just going to stay in a hotel because I don't think my trips up there are going to be enough to justify the cost of keeping a home there."

I smile and take another sip of my beer. Jake has become a permanent full-time resident of Whynot. Apparently, my sister Laken has just that much of an effect on him.

Jake and Lowe lapse into a conversation about the value of real estate in Chicago and I let my gaze drift out across Courthouse Square. To the left of where I sit is Floyd's store, The Reader's Nook, and Central Café. To the right is Sweet Cakes, Trixie's law firm, and Chesty's. On the far side of the courthouse and outside of my view sits Laken's veterinary practice. It hits me all at once that all of my siblings now have their careers and much of their lives tied up right here in the town proper, whereas my life and career is still back at the farm on the outskirts of town.

For the first time in my life, I feel like a bit of an outsider with my brother and sisters. Which is ridiculous because they have never done anything to make me feel that way, and they have always maintained a great deal of interest in the farm even if they don't want to actively be involved in working it.

My gaze starts to drift back over to Sweet Cakes, thinking I might stop in later to see Larkin when my eyes stop on a white sports car parked parallel to the bakery. It's not necessarily the car that gets my attention, even though it's foreign looking and well out of the price range of what someone around here would drive, but rather the man who is leaning against the passenger side and facing Millie's.

He's got his arms crossed over his chest, one leg crossed over the other, and he is staring right at me.

Darby's husband Mitch.

I have no clue how long he has been sitting there clearly with the intent to find me. I know this because his stare is challenging and creepy at the same time. My gut tells me he's probably been there as long as I have been here helping Lowe and Jake move furniture, which has been about an hour. If that's the case, he could have potentially followed me from the farm and I didn't notice.

"Son of a bitch," I mutter. I push up from my rocker and shove my beer at Lowe.

"What?" Lowe says when I start down the porch steps.

"I'll be right back," I call out over my shoulder. Crossing the street, I head toward Mitch.

As I walk his way, I'm secure enough in my manhood that I can admit to the outward appeal this man had to Darby when she was younger. He's good-looking and super successful. While I never asked Darby what he did at the company they had both worked for, the fact he's driving a super expensive car tells me he makes good bank. Why wouldn't that be appealing to a young woman fresh out of college?

Mitch smiles as I draw closer but it's not welcoming. If anything, it's spiteful and his eyes are filled with utter disdain.

I don't mince any words. "What do you want?"

Mitch chuckles and shakes his head at me as if I clearly don't understand why he's here.

I don't.

His arms drop away from his chest, and he casually rests the palms of his hands on the hood of the car he's leaning against.

"I came to give you fair warning," he says with a smirk.

"About what?" I ask.

He smiles again. In a falsely polite and genial voice, he says, "Why... to stay away from my wife, of course."

I am not about to get into it with this man about the nature and extent of my relationship with Darby. It's definitely going places, but it's a journey that's none of his business. But I also don't want to walk away from him right now. I would like to know the extent of his insanity, so I know how to best protect Darby and Linnie.

Because there's no doubt this guy is off his rocker. Darby has told him time and again the marriage is over. She left him and moved away with their daughter. She has rebuffed him every time he has tried to push his way back in. Not only that, I saw firsthand just how nasty he can be and there is no way in hell Darby would go back to that.

While I don't want to goad him into doing something stupid, I do want to know his motivation. "Can I ask you a question?"

He blinks in surprise but then gives me an accommodating smile. "Of course."

"Why do you want a woman who clearly doesn't want you?"

Mitch's face turns red with anger and embarrassment. If looks could kill, I'd be dead in the street right now. He has an answer for me. "Darby doesn't know or understand what she wants or needs. She'll come to her senses soon enough."

"Seems to me she has come to her senses. And the Darby I know has proved to be nothing more than a brilliant woman with a good head on her shoulders. It seems to me she knows exactly what she needs and wants, and it's not you."

Mitch pushes off the car and puffs out his chest. It's comical since he is not a threat to me at all, but I don't go there.

He sneers. "I suppose she needs a man like you? A farmer? You don't know Darby at all. She wants a lifestyle you would never be able to give her."

It just goes to show that Mitch has known Darby for years and I've only known her for weeks, and yet, I know her better than he ever will. Darby doesn't give a crap about lifestyle, fancy cars, or expensive trips. She cares first and foremost that her daughter has everything she needs in life. After that, Darby wants to make her own way. She does not want a man to support her.

There is absolutely no sense in having that conversation with Mitch, though. He doesn't want to know the real Darby. He only wants the woman who used to be content to sit under his thumb. He has no clue that woman is dead and gone.

I casually tuck my hands into the pockets of my jeans, wanting to come off as nonthreatening even though my words are very pointed. "Let me give you a suggestion. You need to leave Darby alone. She's not interested in coming back to you, and she never will be. She is now in a community with many friends who care for and support her. She has everything she needs right here. Do yourself a favor and move on."

Mitch then does something that causes the hair on the back of my neck to stand up. He actually laughs in a maniacal kind of way with something like a high-pitched giggle to it. He wags his finger at me. "You think by going to lunch with my wife and taking her to wedding parties, it gives you knowledge about the real Darby? You don't concern me at all. You're nothing but a speed bump, and I'm going to roll right over you."

Mitch turns his back on me and walks around to the driver side. I don't move an inch as he gets in and slams the door shut. After he turns the car on and puts it in drive, he peels out of his parking spot with a squeal of tires.

After he's out of sight, I head back to Millie's.

Lowe hands me my beer after I jog up the porch steps. "What was that all about?"

"Just had a few things clarified for me," I say before taking a long swallow of the beer.

"What's that?" Jake asks.

"That Darby's soon-to-be ex-husband is a certified nut job. He's also been stalking Darby and me."

"Should you report this to the sheriff?" Lowe asks, his eyebrows drawing inward with worry.

I turn to look at Jake. He knows this guy better than I do. "What do you think?"

Jake's lips press together in a grimace and he shakes his head. "I don't know. Never liked the guy and sort of feel like he's a lot of bluster and no action."

I consider this for a moment. I don't want to be an alarmist and it's probably nothing more than this guy is just a world class jerk. "I think I'll let this ride and I just watch over Darby a little bit closer. Hopefully, he's all hot air."

Hopefully.

CHAPTER 23

Darby

'VE NEVER BEEN to a state fair before. We have them in
Illinois and I'd venture to say they're just as big, if not
bigger, given how important agriculture is to that state. But
the spectacle all around us as we walk over the massive
fairgrounds tells me that the state of North Carolina takes this
fair business very seriously.

I've mostly enjoyed watching Linnie look around with
wide eyes filled with excitement and enthusiasm I just haven't
seen from her in a long time.

Even though I wore my best running shoes complete with
personalized arch supports, my feet are absolutely killing me
from all the walking we did. Not only did we traverse the
midway at least ten times so Linnie could ride the same rides
over and over again, but we had to try all the various foods
being sold.

Crazy food.

Not only do they have the standard fair fare, like funnel
cakes and candied apples, but they have foods that are
particular to the state. I had a little bit of Eastern North
Carolina barbecue—the kind with the vinegar-based sauce—
as well as calabash-style fried seafood.

Then came the really crazy food—much of it deep-fried.
There were fried Twinkies, fried Oreos, and even deep-fried
butter balls. That's right... Frozen balls of butter that were

then coated in batter and deep-fried.

There were pickle popsicles, chocolate-covered bacon, Krispy Kreme hamburgers, and even one vendor truck that boasted chocolate-covered bugs. We avoided that one.

It's late afternoon, and we're all dragging. Colt is gallantly carrying our loot. This includes a bag of gummy bears for Linnie, cotton candy he promised his mama, a goldfish Linnie won tossing Ping-Pong balls into fishbowls, and a huge pink stuffed bear Colt won popping balloons with darts.

"Look… the line for the Ferris wheel isn't long at all," Linnie says with excitement as she points that way.

It's been the one ride she hasn't been on yet but was on her list to try. I silently groan at the thought of waiting for her to ride it. I'm not into the rides at all. No offense to the carnies, but they don't look like the most reliable workers in the world. My luck, I would end up on the ride where an important bolt was misplaced, and I'd be facing imminent death.

I wanted to hold to this philosophy with my daughter and forbid her from going on any of the rides, but I couldn't face her disappointment. So I relented and prayed the entire time she and Colt rode one.

"Okay," I say tiredly. I hold my arms out for Colt to transfer all the stuff to me. "I'll just wait over here."

"You should come on this one with us," Colt says.

I'm shaking my head before the words come out. "No way. Terrified of heights."

And you know, this thing is probably not built very solidly.

"Come on, Mom," Linnie pleads. "Just go on one ride with us. This one is really slow, and I'm sure it's super safe."

There's no way that thing is safe.

But I also see something in Linnie's eyes I used to see a lot but has been a rarity of late. She truly wants to spend quality time with me.

"I have an even better idea," Colt says as he nods to the Ferris wheel. "You two ladies go ride that, and I'm going to sit here and hold on to everything."

"Awesome," Linnie exclaims without even waiting for my agreement that I'd be a willing participant. She grabs my hand and starts pulling me toward the end of the Ferris wheel line. I look over my shoulder helplessly at Colt, who grins at me. He doesn't even look the slightest bit worried I might be marching off to my death.

My stomach rolls the entire time we are waiting, and Linnie just chatters on excitedly about the farm animals we had seen in one of the buildings. She's trying to talk me into some cows and chickens and has promised she will take care of them.

It's not that I doubt her sincerity, but she is only seven and isn't the best on follow through. Still, it might not hurt to get a few chickens. Carlos can easily build us a coop. It would be nice to have fresh eggs each day.

It happens all too quick, but we are now at the front of the line and being ushered into one of the carts. A thin-looking bar is placed over our laps, and Linnie starts rocking the cart back and forth.

"Stop doing that," I say, clutching onto the bar for dear life. We're currently suspended two feet off the ground, yet my pulse has gone through the roof.

Linnie laughs, but she stops the rocking motion. "Sorry, Mom."

She doesn't sound sorry at all.

"I can get off right now, and Colt can get on," I suggest. "He'd be glad to let you rock this back and forth."

"No way," she says. She peels one of my hands off the bar and holds it tightly with hers. "I won't do that anymore. I want to ride this one with you."

That was all I needed to hear from my sweet little girl. A burst of confidence and bravery wells up within me, and I give her hand a squeeze back. Besides, if I'm going to fall to my death, at least it will be doing something that makes my daughter extremely happy.

I gasp when the Ferris wheel goes into motion and we shoot forward and upward a few feet before coming to a stop again, so the next people can be loaded into the cart behind us. I refuse to look down and resolve to look straight out at the horizon.

In order to take my mind off my residual fears, I ask Linnie, "Did you have a good time today, honey?"

Linnie nods. Lifting my arm, she scoots under it, prompting me to cuddle her into my side. "I really did."

"It was nice of Colt to bring us. We should bake a pie for him or something as a thank you."

"My dad's not very nice," Linnie says softly, and I jerk with surprise.

We haven't talked about my last encounter with her dad since the day it happened, when I spent a great deal of time reassuring her that our issues had nothing to do with her.

Because I resolved I would never utter a negative thing about her father—choosing to believe that Linnie is smart enough to figure things out on her own—I steer away from using words like "nice" and "not nice".

Instead, I tell her, "Honey… some people are just built differently. And throughout our lives, we're going to deal with people who may not act the way we wish they would act and who may say things that could be hurtful. I try to let that stuff roll off my back as much as possible. And I hope you can, too."

"Did Dad treat you like that?" she asks.

She's talking about our time together in Illinois for the first seven years of her life. Things gradually got worse over time between Mitch and me, but the one thing I never let happen was letting Linnie see her father and me fighting. Much of this had to do with the fact I would often not argue with Mitch, choosing to take the quieter... more subservient route. Sometimes I regret that, wondering if I should have let her see me stand up to him.

The few times I let my temper get out of control and dared to argue with him, it was always in the confines of our bedroom with the door closed. Linnie had been oblivious to all of it, so watching her father lay into me the other night was an utter shock to her.

Still, I can't answer this question because I don't want to turn her against her dad. If Mitch does that on his own, fine, but my conscience won't let me play a part in it. "Honey... the things that happened between your dad and me are just between us. They have nothing to do with you. That part of Mommy's life is in the past now. The important thing for you to know is I am very happy right now, and that's all that matters."

"I won't have to live with him, will I?" she asks, and my heart breaks from the sound of fear in her voice.

Not because she's afraid of her father, but because she's afraid he has nothing genuine to give her.

And she would be right about that, sadly.

I choose my words carefully because I don't ever want to promise my daughter something I can't deliver. "I will use all of my resources and fight tooth and nail so that doesn't happen. And I'm pretty confident the court would agree you are better off with me. But your father is entitled to visit you. And there are going to be times you're going to have to go with him."

"I know." Her voice is calm, accepting, and so very mature. "I can handle that. I just don't want to live with him full time."

How did my little girl get to be so wise and profound?

Sadly, I suspect she grew up a lot that night Mitch showed up at our house a week ago. While I will always want to protect her from anything ugly, I'm kind of glad she has a little bit of an idea what is going on now.

"I like Colt a lot," Linnie says in an abrupt change of subject. Well, not quite a complete change since she is talking about a man who is part of my life now.

I'm noncommittal. "I like him, too."

"Will you two get married?" she asks innocently.

Out of the mouths of babes.

I lift up my hand that's resting on her shoulder and drag my knuckles across her temple. Leaning over, I give her a kiss on her head. "Baby, it is way too early to be thinking about stuff like that. But we do like each other and as long as you're okay with it, I would like to continue to see Colt."

Linnie pulls back a bit to look at me. "See Colt?"

I laugh and give her a squeeze. "Date Colt. Spend time with him. Get to know him a little better."

"To see if you would like to marry him?" she asks for clarification.

I shake my head and smile. "You only marry for love, Linnie. And that is something that develops between two people over time. I don't know if that will happen between Colt and me, but maybe."

"Did you love Dad?" she asks quietly.

"I did. When I married him, I did."

"So you can stop loving someone?" she asks.

I take a deep breath to get my bearings. It's at this moment I realize we are at the apex of the Ferris wheel. I had been so engrossed in my conversation with my daughter I did not realize we had been continually moving up. My head spins, and I don't know if it's because I'm suspended what seems like a thousand feet in the air or because my daughter has asked me a very complex question about love that's not very easy to answer.

I try my best. "There are many different types of love, Linnie. There is love between a man and a woman, like what your father and I had. There is love between a mother and a daughter. Sometimes the bond is just not strong enough between two people, and love gets sacrificed. The only thing I can tell you is the bond I have with you will never be broken. It would be absolutely impossible for me not to love you."

I know that doesn't answer her question about her father. And she's far too young for me to try to explain to her why I fell out of love with Mitch.

One day, I will tell her all about it. I will do it in a way so as not to disparage her father but rather to hopefully use it as a learning example. To show her that she doesn't need to be controlled by anyone and she should make her own decisions all the time. That when people are in a relationship, they should want each other to be the very best they can be in the way they want to be.

I have so many things I want to teach her, and that is just one of them.

But it's not for today.

CHAPTER 24

Colt

I LOOK ACROSS the table at Darby, who is pouring some ketchup on her plate for her French fries. "Did you have a good time at the game tonight?"

She looks across at me and smiles. "It was awesome. Thank you so much for taking me."

I had a fabulous time at the state fair with Darby and Linnie yesterday. More than anything, I loved learning about the mother-daughter dynamic between the two of them. It was the most loose and relaxed I had seen the pair since they had moved to Whynot, and I think they both needed that.

But as much as I'm going to include Linnie in my plans with her mother, I also want alone time with Darby. I want to get to know her better and let's face it, I want to explore the chemistry we seem to have. When I dropped the girls off yesterday at Farrington Farms, I asked Darby out on a date for the very next night. I was a little concerned it would be too soon and that it was Halloween. I knew it was entirely possibly Darby might have plans to take Linnie trick-or-treating. That was okay... I was prepared to ask her out for the following evening if that was the case.

As it turns out, Jake and Laken were going to take Linnie trick-or-treating outside of Whynot, because there aren't exactly neighborhoods in our area where kids can walk safely down the street. There is the actual town of Whynot, but there's not a lot of people there. Most of the residents live on the outskirts, off dark and windy country roads that are not conducive for trick-or-treating. Trixie and Ry invited Linnie to come trick-or-treating in their neighborhood, which about twenty minutes away. It's a true neighborhood with sidewalks and street lamps to dispel the darkness, and Darby felt that was much safer.

Jake and Laken volunteered to take her and that was that.

When Darby accepted my request for a date, I gave her some options. She could choose which ever one appealed to her the most. The options included going to Clementine's again for dinner, going to see a college basketball game in Chapel Hill, or letting me make dinner for her at my cabin.

While she didn't even raise an eyebrow at the suggestion of coming to my house for dinner—which by the way, was done only with the idea in mind that it would just be dinner—she chose the basketball game as she had never been.

After the game, we were both hungry and decided to get a late-night burger. We chat about the game, and I fill her in on more of the rivalry between Duke and Carolina. Lowe had given me the tickets as he's an alumni of Carolina and didn't feel like going. Said he had too much work to still do at Millie's so it would be ready to open by late November.

"How come you never went to college?" Darby asks while waving a French fry in my direction before popping it in her mouth.

Her curiosity is genuine, and I can tell by the tone of her voice she's not implying my lack of a college education is a negative.

"I knew I would take over the farm," I explain. "It's as simple as that."

Darby circles the tip of her finger over the top of her

water glass. "That's totally legitimate, but you could have gotten some type of degree within the agricultural field to complement things."

"I guess. I mean, looking back on it, I never was a huge fan of school. I made good grades and stuff, but I had so much working knowledge from being out in the fields planting and harvesting since I was probably twelve, it just seemed like a waste of time and money."

Darby nods in agreement. "I think you might be right. You're a smart guy but what more could college teach you that you didn't already figure out on your own or will continue to figure out on your own? I mean, look at you... You figured out how to set up the vineyard and winery."

I chuckle and point my finger teasingly at her. "Well, its success still remains to be seen, but I appreciate your belief in me."

Darby just stares at me a moment, her expression as clear as her eyes are in bright sunlight. She truly does believe in me.

"What about you?" I ask to get the spotlight off of me. "You've got degrees all over the place. What was so important about getting them to you?"

Her finger continues to circle the top of her glass, and she gives a careless shrug. "I guess I was always the brainy nerd who wanted to know how things worked on the microscopic level. It made sense to me to want to be involved on the research side of things. Because I came from a farming background with my family, crop sciences just made the most sense to me."

"So you want to work for a company where you can do research?"

She shrugs again, and her eyes look somewhat troubled. "I thought that's what I wanted. I mean, that's exactly why I'm finishing up my PhD. But Colt… this orchard project has me second guessing that."

"How so?" I ask, putting my forearms on the table and leaning toward her a bit.

She does the same after moving her water glass out of the way. "It kind of feels like my baby. I may not be researching chemical compounds and the makeup of micronutrients, but I am combining those applications to try to figure out how to make a better yield. It's still research in a way, and it feels more personal to me."

"More rewarding?" I ask.

"Yeah. More rewarding."

"So what you're saying is you're considering the potential of staying at Farrington Farms rather than going to work for a big company that deals in crop sciences?" I ask.

She smiles and nods. "I still want to finish my PhD and I can't even begin to finish my thesis for about a year so I can have some good data from what we've already planted. But then, I'll need to make a decision on what to do."

"You have to lay out the pros and cons," I tell her. "We'll get some old-fashioned pen and paper and list it all out one night."

"It's a lot to think about," she says with a sigh. "But I've got nothing but time at this point. I don't have to make the decision any time soon, and I can continue to get settled in at Farrington Farms."

I sit back and settle into the padded bench of the booth we're sitting in, clasping my hands on the table. "The world is your oyster, Darby. You can do whatever you want."

Her pretty face clouds and her eyes darken. She lets her gaze drop to the table. "There was a time in my life that I couldn't do whatever I wanted."

It doesn't take a rocket scientist to figure out she's talking about the years she spent under Mitch's control. I point out, "You're out from under him. It's time to spread your wings."

She slowly lifts her eyes to mine and tilts her head. "You truly mean that, don't you?"

"I'm all about the women's lib, baby," I tell her with a wink.

Darby laughs and shakes her head. "No, you happen to come from a family that is incredibly loyal and supportive to one another. That's all I've ever seen hanging around any of you Mancinkus people. It's just in your nature."

"Well, I'm glad you recognize that, Darby. Because whatever you decide to do or wherever you decide to go, you have my support. Now personally, I'm just going to throw this out there. Selfishly, I'd like you to stay in Whynot and at Farrington Farms. But realistically, you need to go where you have the best opportunity."

"I know," she says softly. "And I'll go ahead and admit to you that one of the main reasons I have considered staying is because of you."

I blink at her in surprise since Darby tends to keep her feelings about our relationship close to the vest. It's obvious there's still a part of her that feels guilty for entering the dating world before she's even fully divorced.

She seems to be embarrassed by that admission, so I rush in with some reassurances. I reach across the table and take one of her hands in mine, sliding my thumb over the ridges of her knuckles. "I'm glad to hear you say that. Because I really like you a lot, Darby. I want to continue to get to know you. I want to see where this goes because I have this feeling deep in my gut that whatever is waiting at the end for us is going to be something beyond my wildest imagination. But I also know you want to take things slow. This is the South, and everything is done slow. Slow is better. It makes every discovery special, so I'm good with that."

Darby's hand tightens around mine. "I'm glad to hear you say those things, but we don't have to take things *that* slow."

Chuckling, I give her a nod. "I'll keep a nicely moderate pace. How does that sound?"

She laughs. "Sounds perfect to me."

"Just remember," I tell her solemnly. "There are no rules we have to follow. So don't let any preconceived ideas of what's appropriate with your separation and divorce come into play. You've answered the biggest question I have and that's if you're truly over your husband and your marriage. I know you are, and that's all that matters to me."

Darby sighs and pulls her hand away from me. She uses it to tuck her hair behind her ear before resting her chin in the palm of her hand to stare across the table at me. "I hate we even have to talk about Mitch when we're talking about our relationship."

I shrug before once again settling casually back into the bench. "He's always going to be a part of your life because he's Linnie's dad. It just sucks the current context of what we have to discuss about him has nothing to do with his role as a father."

"I hate he's making things so difficult."

I stare at Darby for a moment, weighing the indecision that's been plaguing me the last few days. I have not told her about my run-in with Mitch on Saturday outside of Millie's, since I didn't want to bring up any unnecessary drama regarding her husband. But I also can't let go of the fact I suspect the guy is slightly unhinged.

"Can I ask you a personal question about your marriage?"

To my relief and satisfaction, Darby immediately answers, "Anything."

"Did he ever physically hurt you?"

She shakes her head. "No. Mitch was always most vicious with his words."

"I just want you to be careful around him," I tell her carefully. "I saw the way he reacted to you standing up to him that day, and he's not used to that. There's no telling what he could do."

Darby nods. "I hear you. And I agree... Mitch can be unpredictable."

"Have you heard from him?" I ask.

"Nope. But Jake did find me an attorney in Raleigh who's going to take the case."

"That's good."

Darby sits straight up in her chair and slaps her palms on the table, causing me to jump slightly. She gives me a brilliant smile and declares, "Enough talk about Mitch. Let's talk about dessert."

I laugh and look around for our waiter. Dessert is an excellent idea.

I wonder what chocolate will taste like on her lips.

CHAPTER 25

Darby

LINNIE LAYS DOWN a yellow zero on top of my red zero and shouts, "Uno."

She's bouncing up and down on her seat at the kitchen table, barely able to contain her excitement.

The play passes to Colt, who studies the four cards in his hand. He grimaces, pulls out a yellow five, and then lays it down.

It's my turn, and I don't need to look hard at the two cards left in my hand. I have neither a five nor a yellow card, so I pull one from the draw pile.

My eyes sparkle with competition. I give a smug smile to Linnie before dropping a blue five on top.

Her smile back is ten times more smug than my own. She drops a green five, and I groan.

"I win," she yells, throwing her hands up in victory before dropping one of them to push her glasses up her nose.

Colt throws his cards down in frustration and looks at me. "It's unnatural how often she wins this game. That right there was just creepy that she had a three in her hand. If I didn't know any better, I would say she was cheating."

"Let's play again," Linnie says as she starts gathering all the cards in.

"Oh no, you don't," I tell her sternly as I pull the cards out of her hands. "It's eleven o'clock, and we said that last round was the final hand. It is way past your bedtime, pipsqueak."

I get a long, drawn out, "M-o-o-o-m-m."

I shake my head, pointing to the doorway that leads from the kitchen to the staircase. "Upstairs now. Get your teeth brushed, your jammies on, and your booty into bed."

Linnie huffs with frustration, but she's also a sweetly obedient kid. She pushes from the chair and looks across the table at Colt. "Goodnight. See you tomorrow?"

Colt smiles at my daughter, and it makes my heart trip a beat. "You got it, sugar."

Somewhere during one of the early hands of Uno, Linnie had talked Colt into taking her fishing tomorrow. I was invited along, but I don't do slimy fish.

Linnie turns to me and asks, "Will you tuck me in?"

A surge of tenderness overwhelms me that Linnie still wants me to do something as simple yet needful as tucking her into bed. I get up and say, "Of course I will, kiddo. Let's go."

Colt stands up from the table and says, "I better get going."

I shake my head and give him a sly wink. "Don't go just yet. I'll be right back down."

Colt's eyebrows rise, and the look of interest on his face only makes him look infinitely more handsome. Knowing he is interested in me on a more intimate level gives me butterflies in my stomach.

Linnie and I trudge up the stairs hand in hand. She chatters away about fishing and pesters me about going to look for chickens. I help her get undressed and slip her nightgown over her head. Linnie crawls into bed, grabs her favorite stuffed animal, which is a beaten-up old brown bear she's had since she was a baby. She tucks it in close and turns on her side, looking up at me. "Mom… are you going to kiss Colt tonight?"

My jaw drops, and I stare aghast at my daughter. "Why would you ask something like that? You're only seven—what do you know about kissing?"

Linnie rolls her eyes, meaning my daughter must know more than I give her credit for. Regardless, I shut the conversation down. I had indeed thought about kissing Colt before he left, but I don't want my daughter thinking about it.

Pulling the covers up to her chin, I lean over and press my lips to her forehead. "You're far too young to worry about kissing."

Linnie giggles. In a singsongy voice, she says "Mommy and Colt, sitting in a tree, K-I-S-S-I-N-G."

Standing up straight, I give my daughter a chastising look, but turn away from her before I start laughing. I walk to her doorway and before I turn the light off, I glance back at her. She's so precious laying there staring at me with a sweet smile on her face and a heart full of love.

"Good night, baby."

"Good night, Mom," she says. "I love you."

"I love you, too."

My old Linnie is completely back, and nothing in this world makes me happier.

Back downstairs, I find Colt sitting in the living room on one end of the couch. He grins when I come off the bottom step and pats the seat beside him. Shooting me a mischievous grin, he murmurs in a wickedly sexy voice, "Want to come sit beside me and make out for a little bit?"

I put my hand to my mouth, giving him a quick look as I tilt my head and bat my eyelashes. "Why, Mr. Mancinkus… you're being very bold."

"You like me being bold," he asserts confidently in a low voice, no trace of humor at all. He holds his hand out. "Come here, Darby."

There's no controlling my feet as I start walking toward him without hesitation. His eyes shimmer in the glow of the table lamp beside him. The minute I place my fingertips against the palm of his hand, I feel that electric snap of recognition and attraction shoot through me.

I put one knee to the couch cushion beside his hip and bring my lips right to his. Somehow, he turns my body so I end up sitting across his lap. It puts me in the perfect position for him to kiss me deeply. More intimately than he has ever kissed me before, even the night he took me to the Carolina basketball game and walked me up to my door. That night we had made out for a few minutes before I went inside, but this is completely different.

Something about sitting on a couch across his lap, knowing it would be very easy for us to just lay down on the couch to make out, which could possibly lead to all kinds of hot and bothering things that we have no business doing with my daughter in her room just up those stairs, makes me doubt what we're doing.

As if Colt had a peek inside my mind and knew in this moment I was thinking of my daughter, he grips my hair at the back of my head and pulls me gently away. "This was probably a bad idea."

"I know we said we were going to move slowly, but I really am not feeling like going slow right now."

"Me either," he admits in a gruff voice. "Which is really why you need to get off my lap."

I giggle as he takes me by my hips and sets me on the cushion beside him. He takes my hand in his, and we both kick our feet up on the coffee table, staring at nothing.

"You have a really great kid," Colt says to break the silence. "You've done a remarkable job raising her so far."

I give a mirthless laugh. "I sure as heck didn't feel like that when we first arrived in Whynot. She was so angry at me that I was afraid I wouldn't reach her."

I roll my head on the cushion to look at Colt. He mimics my actions, and our eyes lock. "I don't think I would've gotten through to her as quickly if it wasn't for you," I tell him solemnly. "That day you took her horseback riding was when it all changed. As her mother, I just didn't think about something as simple as giving my daughter back something she really loved."

Colt smiles and then leans over to give me a very soft, brief kiss on my lips. "You would have figured it out sooner rather than later."

"I'd like to kiss you again," I tell him with an impish grin.

Colt gives me a wicked smile. "Kissing again would be really good. And we can't get into too much trouble sitting side by side."

Our bodies start leaning in toward each other, and my eyes drop to his mouth as it gets closer. I raise a hand and place my fingertips against his jaw, which is prickly with a five o'clock shadow.

Just before our mouths touch, Colt's phone starts ringing.

He mutters a curse and pulls his phone out, disconnecting the call and sending it to voicemail without even looking at the screen. Setting the phone down on the coffee table, he turns back toward me and says, "Let's try that again."

We don't even have time to move toward each other before his phone starts ringing again. Colt frowns and grabs it off the table, turning it to look at the screen. "It's my dad. Let me get this."

"Of course."

Colt connects the call and places the phone to his ear. "What's up, Dad?"

I have no clue what's being said on the other end, but Colts entire demeanor changes. He stands suddenly from the couch, and his eyes go dead. "I'm on my way."

I jump up, knowing that something awful has happened. Given that Colt's father is the one who called, I immediately suspect something happened to his mother.

"What's wrong?" I ask as I reach out and touch his arm.

Colt only spares me a quick glance. "The vineyard is on fire."

"What?" I yell in surprise.

"I gotta go," he says as he starts toward the door.

"Let me get Linnie and we'll come with you," I call after him.

He yells back without even sparing me a glance. "No time."

And then he's gone out the door with the screen door slamming shut behind him. For a moment, I'm stunned to inaction, but then I think about that dead look in Colt's eyes and my feet are moving. I run up the stairs and burst into the Linnie's room.

When I flip on the light, she sits straight up in bed. "I'm sorry, honey... but I need you to get up and get dressed. We have to go out to Mainer Farms."

"What happened?" she asks as she jumps out of bed and starts frantically pulling her nightgown off.

I grab the clothes we had taken off her earlier from the hamper and toss them her way. "Colt's vineyard is on fire. We're going to go out there and see if we can help."

She doesn't ask any further questions, but jumps quickly into action, getting dressed faster than I've ever seen my daughter move in my life.

It seems to take forever to drive out to Mainer Farms. My heart sinks when I see a red glow in the distance against the night sky as we make our way down the bumpy farm road that leads straight to the vineyard.

As we come over a ridge, I gasp at the eerie sight before us. Several acres of the vineyard are on fire. It looks to be the wooden trellises blazing, but the heat from those flames has got to be singeing and killing the actual vines.

Colt planted ten acres, and I would guess about a quarter of it is on fire.

He doesn't have a quarter of his vineyard to spare to such a needless loss.

I put my car in park, reminding myself for the hundredth time I need to get a work truck, and Linnie and I both jump out. My eyes lock on Colt, who is standing with both of his hands placed on top of his head. He's staring blankly at the inferno before him.

I also see his mother and father, Lowe and Mely, as well as Jake and Laken. Everyone is standing around helplessly because there's nothing that can be done without a water source. Vaguely, I hear in the distance the sound of sirens coming, but the most the fire department will be able to do is to contain the blaze from spreading. There is no saving what's already on fire.

"Mom... what happened?" Linnie asks softly as she slides her hand into mine.

I can't tear my eyes away from the blazing vineyard. "I don't know."

CHAPTER 26

Colt

THE SUN FINALLY breaks over the edge of the pine trees that border the end of the vineyard, casting an almost mystical orange glow over the land. Three solid rows of vines went up in flames last night. Stretching a couple of hundred yards back to the tree line, I can see nothing but the blackened T-shaped trellises looking like a row of crucifixion crosses. Not only were the trellises destroyed, but the vines in between were charred beyond saving.

Picking up my thermos of coffee sitting beside me on the tailgate of my truck where I'm sitting, I take a sip. I didn't get a minute of sleep last night after the fire department and the sheriff left. I was heartsick over what had happened, and I took it out directly on Darby. She had shown up last night with Linnie out of pure concern for me. And when she asked me how she could help, I only told her that she needed to go home because there was nothing she could do.

The vineyard was beyond a mere offer of help.

Her face crumpled because her offer had nothing to do with the burning vineyard but rather it was an offer of emotional support, and I had turned my nose up at it.

Last night, I wasn't thinking clearly at all. I know I need to apologize to her for my behavior.

After everyone left, I went to my cabin and took a hot shower. It seemed that no matter how hard I scrubbed, I couldn't get rid of the smell of charred wood and ashes. I laid on my bed all night staring at the ceiling, trying to figure out how I could potentially recover from this. The economic losses were insurmountable in my opinion, and there's no way I'll be able to replace what we lost.

My thoughts went even darker as I laid awake. It seemed to me this was an ominous sign that perhaps I had no business squandering that grant on a pipe dream. Even darker yet, my mind suggested I was not the person who needed to be running Mainer Farms.

The sound of an approaching truck catches my attention, and I look over my shoulder. It's Sheriff Brown's old Ford Bronco bumping down the dirt road toward me.

Sheriff Ollie Brown is actually a Yankee transplant down here, same as Pap. He retired from a small police department in New Hampshire, and he and his wife came down South for better weather. It appears he wasn't all that ready to give up law enforcement because he ran for sheriff about fifteen years ago and won the election hands down. He's run unopposed since then because everyone knows he can't be beat. He is a tough but fair lawman, and he's respected by everyone around these parts. Since Mainer Farms is outside the Whynot city limits, the Sheriff's department will be investigating.

Ollie parks next to my truck. When he gets out, I see he has two cups of coffee from Central Café. Even though they have lids on them, the fall air is chilly enough I can see the hot steam coming out of the small openings on top.

"Morning, Colt." He hands me one of the cups, and I open my thermos to pour it in.

"Ollie," I acknowledge his greeting.

"Got some information for you," he says, and my head jerks up in surprise. When Ollie was out here last night writing up an arson and vandalism report, he didn't think we would have much luck in catching the perpetrator. This part of the farm is well off the beaten path, and anyone could stealthily drive down here to sabotage the vineyard.

Ollie plops down on the tailgate beside me and says, "Do you know a Mitch McCulhane?"

I'd like to say his name surprises me, but it doesn't. I'd like to say I never once considered him, but I did. In fact, Mitch was the only person I could think who had enough malice to do something like this. The only problem was I couldn't figure out how he could pull it off. There's no way that city-slicking corporate type with his fancy sports car and three-hundred-dollar loafers would be able to set a vineyard on fire.

"Yeah. I know him." I purposely leave out Darby's name and how I know him, although Ollie probably knows. There's not much that slips by him. The way the gossip mill operates in this town, there are probably not many people who don't know I'm seeing Darby.

I don't say her name, though, because it actually hurts a little. Knowing I hurt her last night when I brushed her off and knowing this is about to get very, very complicated.

"What did you find?"

Ollie takes off his cream-colored Stetson with the sheriff's badge pinned to the front. He scratches his head before putting the hat back on. "It appears Floyd did a little investigating of his own last night."

Floyd had come out last night as the vineyard was burning, but he didn't stay long. In fact, I remember him saying something like, "I've got something I gotta do."

"What did Floyd find out?" I ask.

The sheriff's body shakes with amused laughter for a

moment, and he looks at me with a smirk. "Turns out he had been in Chesty's at the time the fire was being set. He remembers just before getting the call about what happened, that Travis Robbins and Gil Ellis came into the bar and they were already drunk."

"Typical for those boys," I observe.

Ollie nods. "Floyd distinctly remembers that both boys smelled like gasoline. Once he got out to the vineyard and saw what happened, he connected the dots. Went back into the bar, hauled those boys out by the scruffs of their necks, and held them by shotgun until I arrived."

My eyes go wide, and my jaw drops open. "You're kidding me?"

"Nope. Not kidding you. I took them into the station to question them, and they both admitted to doing it."

My brows draw inward, totally confused. "What does that have to do with Mitch?"

"The boys claim they were hired to do it for a thousand dollars each. They don't know the guy's name, but they described Mitch to a T. Of course, I only know who Mitch is from Floyd. He helped me connect the rest of it up, and I figure this Mitch guy has a bone to pick with you since you're dating Darby."

I shake my head in disbelief. Travis and Gill would definitely have the ability to set the vineyard on fire. In fact, the tire tracks we found running down the rows indicated it was probably somebody with a large barrel filled with gas and a sprayer attachment that let them put out so much fuel over such a large area. Once they got it sprayed down, it was simply a matter of tossing a match on it and watching it burn.

"We've arrested both boys," Ollie tells me gravely. "I've got men out trying to find Mitch to bring him in for questioning. I expect he's going to deny it and he paid them boys cash, so there's no trail."

"Is that going to be enough to arrest him?" I ask.

"That's going to be up to the prosecutor," Ollie says with a sigh "But I don't see why not. Those two boys' testimony is evidence. It would be up to a jury to figure it all out."

I nod, letting my gaze wander back over the burned rows of trellises. Those vines hadn't even had a chance to prosper. All because some nut job was jealous of me seeing his soon-to-be ex-wife.

It just doesn't make any sense, and I'm having a hard time wrapping my head around it.

Ollie claps me on the back before hopping off the tailgate. "Just wanted to tell you the news in person. I'll fill you in after we've talked to Mitch."

"Thanks, Sheriff. I appreciate it."

I sit out on my tailgate long after Ollie leaves and finish my coffee. I do a lot of thinking.

Around eight o'clock, I get in my truck and head over to Farrington Farms.

I need to talk to Darby.

◆

I NO MORE get pulled in front of Darby's house and turn my truck off before she is walking out the front door and down the porch steps to greet me. She must have been near the kitchen window and heard me pull up.

She looks concerned for me and wary all at the same time.

I get out of the truck and wait for her to come to me. It's better we have this conversation out here where Linnie can't hear it.

"You haven't been returning my texts or calls," she says

with a hint of accusation in her tone.

I rub my hand across my jaw and give her an apologetic look. "Yeah... I'm sorry about that. Also for the way I blew you off last night. I just had a lot on my mind."

A look of utter relief breaks across her face, and it makes my guts twist I'm getting ready to cause her anxiety again. "Listen... Darby... Sheriff Brown has found out who set the vineyard on fire."

The expression of relief on her face matches the tone of her voice. "That's wonderful news."

There's no sugarcoating what I have to tell her, so I don't. "It was Mitch. He hired two local boys to go out and do it."

Darby's face drains of all color, her hand covering her mouth in shock. "Oh, God."

"Sheriff Brown has got his guys out looking for Mitch right now. They're going to bring him in for questioning, but they've already arrested the two guys who admitted to doing it. I expect Mitch is going to be arrested as well."

Darby's eyes cut over to the farmhouse before coming back to me, "Maybe they're lying. I just can't imagine Mitch doing something like that."

A wave of white-hot anger floods through me that she would even think to defend the man. "How could you think he wouldn't do it?" I ask bitterly. "He's a nut job. He's completely obsessed with you, and doesn't want anyone else to have you."

Either she doesn't recognize that the anger in my voice is directed at her or she's not thinking straight because she gives a shake of her head and says, "It's just so out of character for him. And what would it accomplish?"

I growl in frustration. "Come on, Darby... Crazy people don't need motivation other than they are crazy."

She blinks in surprise, taking a step backward from the fury in my voice. "I'm sorry. I don't mean to be defending him. This is just a shock, and I don't even know how to go about telling our daughter that her father may have been involved in something like that."

"Was involved in something like that," I correct her. "Not may have been. *Was*."

Darby seems to understand at this point that my anger is multi-focused. She straightens her spine and asks me point blank, "Are you blaming me for any of this? Because you seem to be directing some of that anger toward me."

I sigh as I give a slow shake of my head. "No. I'm not blaming you. I am blaming myself for not taking him seriously, but none of this is your fault, Darby. I swear to you."

"I'm just trying to understand this," she says, her voice sounding lost and unsure.

"He approached me last Saturday when I was helping Lowe and Jake move furniture into Millie's. He was making some veiled threats."

"Why didn't you tell me?" she demands angrily. "I could have confronted him."

I throw my hands out in frustration. "I don't know. I didn't want to worry you. I didn't think he would do something so heinous. Like you, I didn't think he'd come after me in such a criminal way."

Darby takes a few steps back, putting her hand over her mouth again. Her eyes are wide and frightened. She glances back to the house again and murmurs, "How am I going to explain this to Linnie? She's going to be so confused."

This is the part that kills me. That I could possibly be hurting Linnie with my decision.

"I'm going to make sure that Mitch is prosecuted to the fullest extent of the law," I tell her softly, but my words almost seem to knock her over. She turns her gaze to me, and it kills me how bleak it is. "It's not going to bring back what I lost, but I need the justice. I hope you can understand that, Darby."

Darby's expression is troubled when she nods. Her voice is soft. "Of course. I understand."

I take a step toward her, bringing my hand up to her face. It should be a reassuring touch, but it's really nothing more than a goodbye. "This complicates things too much, Darby. I think we need to take a break."

Her eyes widen, and her voice is accusing. "You said you weren't blaming me."

"I'm not," I assure her. "But I'm getting ready to go after your husband. And I know he's not really your husband in truth, but he is in name and that makes things very messy. Let's not forget... he's Linnie's dad. I really don't think either of you need the man trying to bring her father down in your life right now."

If I expected Darby to fight to keep this relationship going, I would be sorely disappointed. She takes a step back from me and nods. Her voice is clear and strong. "I understand."

And then she turns away from me and walks back into the house.

CHAPTER 27

Darby

I'M LUCKY TO find a parallel parking spot in front of Central Café. Not only is it the height of the breakfast rush because most of the court personnel are rushing in to grab sausage biscuits and such, but a very important meeting has been set up to be held here this morning.

I check traffic in my side mirror. When I see it's clear, I open the door and get out of my old BMW.

I really have to get a farm truck.

Especially after calling this meeting this morning. That's because today I am establishing my foothold in this community.

"What's up, Farmer Darby?" I hear as I shut the door.

I look over the sidewalk to see Larkin walking my way. She was invited to the meeting as well.

"Hey," I call.

When she reaches me, she surprises me by giving me a long, hard hug. "How are you doing, my friend?"

I squeeze her hard and pull back. "I'm hanging in there as best I can."

Larkin is fully up to speed on what's happened the last two days since the fire, and that's because she was at my house last night, drinking wine and commiserating.

Giving me the type of support a really good friend does. It was much needed because in just two days, Colt's vineyard was partially destroyed, he broke things off with me, and my soon-to-be ex-husband was arrested and charged along with the other two men he hired.

"Mitch got out easily on bail," I tell her. That had happened this morning. The only reason I know this is because Floyd called to tell me. I'm not even sure how he got my cell number.

"How's Linnie taking it?" she asks.

I shrug. Linnie's confused and hurt and angry and well… her emotions, like mine, are all over the place. What we decided last night when I tucked her into bed was that we are just going to take each day as it came and trust in the justice system to work. Thankfully, Linnie never asked me if I thought her father did it because I would have had to tell her I thought he had.

"We better get inside," I say as I point at the cafe.

"I can't wait to see what you have on tap for this meeting," she says. She hooks her arm through mine, and we walk to the door together.

She knows I have something up my sleeve to help Colt, but she doesn't know the details. I've only shared those with two people… Catherine and Jerry Mancinkus.

"You're just going to have to wait a few more minutes," I tease.

"I think I have a sneaking suspicion what you might do," she says confidently. And she probably does. Larkin is the one I poured my heart out to after Colt said he wanted to break things off. She knows very well what I feel for her brother.

A huge, growling rumble fills the air around me, and I can feel the vibration of a motorcycle approaching. Larkin and I turn around to see a massive Harley-Davidson slowly coming our way. It's all black and chrome, but the most distinguishing feature is the man riding it. He's dressed all in black. Black leather chaps, black leather motorcycle jacket, and one of those black helmets that cover just the top portion of the head. He has black sunglasses on, black gloves, and black boots.

"Oh my God," Larkin breathes out the side of her mouth. "It's Jax Teller from *Sons of Anarchy*."

I snicker, but I couldn't agree more with her. The man has longish golden-blond hair and a neatly trimmed blond beard. No clue what color his eyes are, but his facial features are model perfect with the straight nose and hard jaw. About the only difference between him and Jax is this guy looks to be a lot bigger. He's tall and really built. It's obvious even under all that leather he's wearing.

The motorcycle slows to a stop in the street right beside where we stand on the sidewalk, and Larkin self-consciously starts tugging at the short ends of her hair at the nape of her neck.

The man cuts the motorcycle off and removes his glasses. Larkin and I both suck in air when we are blindsided with dazzling green eyes that are crinkling at the corners as the man smiles at us.

"Morning, ladies," he says in a gruff, gravelly voice that sends shivers up my spine. This man is way too good looking for words.

The man gives me a polite smile before turning his attention to Larkin. Her cheeks turn pink when he runs an appreciative look over her before asking, "Can you recommend a good place to stay in this town?"

Larkin doesn't say anything. A glance at her shows she seems to be frozen in place, staring at the man. I give her a nudge in the ribs with my elbow, and she snaps out of it.

Her hand comes up to play with her hair again as she says, "Um... we don't have anything open right now. I mean, we used to have a bed-and-breakfast called Millie's. It's right over there. But Millie's sons are a bunch of drunken losers, and they let it get run into the ground with termite infestations. But someone bought it. And then sold it to my sister-in-law. Her name's Mely. And her husband... that's my brother Lowe... made all the repairs. And they just moved in furniture. But it's not going to be open for a few weeks yet. And I'm rambling."

The man grins at Larkin, showing straight white teeth. "I think your rambling is cute. What's the closest town that will have lodging?"

"That would be Milner," Larkin says, her voice a little steadier. "Just keep straight on this road out of town and you'll run into it."

The man studies Larkin for a moment before giving her a nod. "Much obliged. Maybe I'll come back sometime and check out Millie's once it opens."

Larkin blushes and ducks her head. Her words come out stammering again. "That would be okay... nice. I mean... cool, I guess."

The man chuckles and says, "Totally cute."

He starts the motorcycle back up, the rumble of it vibrating the sidewalk, and slowly rolls out of town. We watch him until he disappears. Even after he's gone, I have to bump my hip against Larkin's to get her attention.

She turns to me and gives a low whistle. "He was totally hot."

"You were totally a babbling cutie pie," I tease.

Larkin laughs at herself. "I've never been the best around super good-looking men."

"Well, if he does come back to town, you better practice on your communication skills because that man had serious interest in you."

We start toward Central Café and walk up to the door. Larkin opens it and motions me in.

The sound of several people chattering hits me, and I'm surprised to see it's standing room only inside. Every table and stool at the counter is taken and all the spots in between are filled with standing people. It seems the entire town has turned out for this meeting.

I see Billy Crump standing next to an older man who has to be his father. Judge Bowe is sitting at the counter next to Pap with a plate of biscuits and gravy in front of him. There's Floyd, Jason, and Della. Mary Margaret Quinn, who owns the antique shop, smiles at me. I see Sissy Givens, who owns Lady Marmalade's sitting next to her. In the corner sitting at one of the larger tables is the Mancinkus clan. Jerry and Catherine as well as Laken, Lowe, Mely, and Jake. Trixie and Ry are sitting there as well, and Larkin walking in behind me completes the package. There's only one person missing, which is Colt, but he wasn't invited to this meeting.

I survey the room. There are dozens of other people here who I don't know. They were all invited through the grapevine.

I walk through the crowd which starts quieting down as all eyes turn to me. I make my way over to Catherine and Jerry and they both stand to give me a hug.

To stop the remaining chatter, Muriel stands on top of the counter and gives a shrill whistle. Everyone quiets and turns to her. "All right, everyone… You were invited here for a meeting by that woman over there, Darby McCulhane. Now some of you know her, but those who don't, you need to know she's sweet on Colt Mancinkus and he's sweet on her."

All eyes turn toward me, and I flush with embarrassment. I was never very good at speaking in front of a lot of people, and Muriel just called me out as "being sweet on Colt".

Muriel continues. "She's got something important to say, so everybody shut up and listen."

There's a slight chittering of laughter before it goes quiet.

I clear my throat and take in a breath. "Thank you, everyone, for coming out here this morning. If you don't know already, I'm the operations manager at Farrington Farms. While I'm new to your community, I have been welcomed so graciously I feel like I'm an absolutely accepted member here."

I feel Catherine's hand go to my lower back for support.

I continue. "As you all know, three nights ago, Mainer Farms was viciously attacked. The new vineyard Colt had planted was sabotaged. Part of it was sprayed with gas and lit on fire."

"Evil is what it was," someone in the crowd mutters.

There are murmurs of agreement rippling throughout.

When I hold my hands up, the room goes silent again. I take a moment to let my gaze sweep the room before I say, "It's time for this community to come together. The first step is Farrington Farms and Mainer Farms are going to enter into a little business venture together. You all know Jake by now, and he's going to invest some money into the Mainer's new winery. This will help to repair some of the damage that was done. But we need more. We need immediate action to remove all the burned timber and vines to get it rebuilt again as quickly as possible. That's what I'm here for today... to ask for your help."

Unsurprisingly, Floyd is the first to stand up. "I'll do whatever you want, Darby. I'll also donate some of the supplies to build new trellises."

I give Floyd a grateful smile. "Thanks, Floyd."

A man in his early sixties stands up from one of the tables. "My name is Silas Goddard. I own one of the competing farms. But I've got some IOUs from one of the local nurseries. I'll call that in to get some new vines, or at least whatever I can."

I incline my head and say, "That's very sweet, Mr. Goddard."

After that, there's a period of several minutes where people are calling out what they want to do to help. Mostly it's nothing more than volunteering their hands and their backs for labor. Muriel offers to cater food. Laken stands up and wrangles a deal with Eustace Roop, who apparently has the best organic compost in the county. She traded veterinarian services for Eustace's goats in exchange for the compost.

I sat there and watched as every single person in that diner, young or old, volunteered in some way to help get Colt and Mainer Farms back on their feet. It was perhaps the most amazing event I have ever witnessed. I never knew there was such collective goodness in people.

If I had had any doubt about where Linnie and I should set down our roots, it was obliterated in this moment.

I let Catherine and Jerry take over from there, as they are going to coordinate the efforts to get the winery and vineyard reestablished. My work was done.

CHAPTER 28

Colt

G RABBING AN APPLE, I give one last look around my kitchen and ensure it's completely tidied up. I never walk out the door to start my day unless my bed is made and the kitchen is clean from whatever mess I might make at breakfast. The making the bed came from my drill instructor dad and the tidy kitchen from my mama.

I walk out of my cabin with a surprising spring in my step. When I woke up this morning, I decided it was time to take the bull by the horns and start rebuilding. For the last few days, I'll admit I spent part of that time feeling sorry for myself. Some of that time I spent trying to make an alternate plan that would not rely on a winery to stabilize Mainer Farms. And part of the time, I thought about Darby and the fact I pushed her away because her husband torching my grapes just complicated things.

Mitch had indeed been questioned, arrested, and subsequently let out on bail, which he easily came up with. It appears the prosecuting attorney—who I met with yesterday—decided Gil and Travis made credible enough witnesses to charge Mitch as well. But that wasn't the most important thing that happened at that meeting. And when I walked out, I was satisfied justice would be carried out in a way that was palatable to everyone.

I jump in my truck to head over to the vineyard. I would

ordinarily take the Gator, but I plan on heading over to Farrington Farms after. Right now, my goal is to take an inventory of what needs to be replaced so I can get supplies ordered. The more important goal today, though, is to talk to Darby to see if we can work things out. I may not have things quite figured out with the farm, but the one thing I know for sure is I don't want to give up what I've built with her so far. I'll be darned if I'm going to let her psycho soon-to-be ex-husband ruin things for us. And while I do believe part of his plan to torch my vineyard was retaliatory, I also think he did it hoping to cause a rift between Darby and me. He succeeded for all of about five minutes, but no more.

I bump along the dirt road, humming a tune along with the radio. When I crest the ridge and the vineyard comes into view, I slam on the brakes of my truck so hard I skid slightly sideways. There are people swarming the rows of vines with vehicles parked all over the place around the edges of the field. "What in the hell?"

I shake my head and hit the gas, driving another two hundred yards where I park beside Floyd's truck. Hopping out, I take a more scrutinized look around. It seems like the entire town of Whynot is standing in my backyard so to speak. Muriel has two long tables set up with food, and a big commercial-sized thermos of what I'm betting is coffee. She's handing out wrapped breakfast sandwiches with a smile. Floyd is down one of the rows directing a truck laden with timbers. Several of the townsfolk are there waiting to unload.

Lowe and Jake are working with about ten other men to take down the wires on the trellises that have been burnt, and Pap sits nearby on a folding chair yelling out instructions to people.

I even see Morri D ridiculously dressed in a pair of

patchwork overalls and a big wide-brimmed hat to shade his face from the sun. He's passing out water bottles to people.

And I see Linnie. Sweet little Linnie pulling charred vines out of the ground. How in the world can I even face that kid with her father being arrested at my direction?

My gaze sweeps left and right, searching for the one person I haven't seen, and... there she is.

Darby.

Kneeling in the dirt where one of the vines has recently been pulled out. She's got a kit, and she's testing my soil. No doubt she's got a truck somewhere around here laden with micronutrients to spray once she gets results.

A hand claps down on my shoulder, and I turn my head to find my father standing there. "About time you joined us."

"What the heck is going on?" I ask.

My dad points over to Darby, who has yet to see me, and says, "Your girl organized this. Called together a town meeting. She got people to volunteer time and some supplies to get what was lost replaced."

My eyes go wide, and the most unusual feeling of wonder and humility flows through me that someone could care that much about me.

Here I was, the man who pushed her away because things got a little messy, and she is riding in on a white horse to save the day.

Amazing.

"Excuse me, Dad," I mutter as I head toward Darby. The sound of my dad's laughter follows me.

I walk past people who smile and give me encouraging words. I shake hands and clap backs, saying "thank you" a dozen times before I reach Darby.

When I walk up behind her, the only clue I'm approaching is when my shadow reaches her before I do. She cranes her neck to look over her shoulder, and her eyes widen with surprise when she sees me.

I simply walk around her, and then drop to my knees in the dirt right in front of her. Grabbing her face with my hands, I pull her roughly into me for a hard kiss. I release her, look deeply into her eyes, and murmur, "You are incredible, and I don't deserve you."

She gives me a shy smile. In a self-deprecating tone, she says, "I just organized. Everybody else who turned out here to work are the incredible ones."

I kiss her hard again. When I pull back this time, I say, "You did all of this for me? After I told you that we needed to take a break?"

She gives me a tiny nod.

I kiss her hard for a third time, and I don't pull away this time. Instead, I tilt my head and deepen the kiss until her arms snake around my neck and mine go around her back to pull her to me. I vaguely hear a few people whistle and someone yells, "Get a room," but I don't care.

Everyone can just watch and behold the power that Darby McCulhane has over me.

When I pull back this time, I know I have to say the right words to put everything back on track. "Darby… I'd been thinking I was falling in love with you over the last few weeks. But right now, I am absolutely certain of it. And I don't want to stop the fall. I was wrong to ask for a break. I don't care about Mitch or what he's done. If you and Linnie will have me, I would like to start seeing you again."

Darby doesn't respond, but just stares at me for a few painful moments. I think she may be on the verge of telling me to go to hell—which would be unacceptable to me—when she puts her palms to my cheeks. "I think I'm falling in love with you, too. And I wasn't really going to let you break things off. I had a plan."

"You did, did you?" I ask with a skeptical eyebrow cocked.

She nods, bringing her face closer to mine. "But that plan is not needed now since you came to your senses."

I stand up from the ground, pulling Darby up with me. "Listen... There's something I need to tell you about what I did yesterday."

Darby tilts her head. "You can tell me anything."

This I know, but it's still nice to hear. "I met with the prosecutor yesterday. Travis, Gill, and Mitch have all hired attorneys. They approached the prosecutor with plea deals, and he wanted my opinion on what to do."

"Oh," Darby says softly.

"I told the prosecutor to cut deals that did not involve any jail time. I just couldn't be a part of putting Linnie's dad in jail. I think he deserves it, but I just couldn't do it."

"You didn't have to do that, Colt. Linnie and I would have dealt with the fallout from Mitch's actions. I want you to have the justice that you deserve."

I chuckle and scratch the back of my neck before admitting. "I'll get justice. Part of the plea deal is Mitch has to pay full restitution for the damages. I'll be able to pay back all these people who donated supplies."

Darby tilts her head back and gives a delighted laugh. "Hit Mitch in his purse strings. That will really hurt him."

"Have you heard from him?" I ask, and her laughter dies.

Darby shakes her head. "As soon as he made bail, he slunk back to Illinois. His divorce attorney contacted mine and said the divorce proceedings would be back on through Illinois, which is really good news since it won't take that long to finalize things."

"That's terrific news."

Darby's eyes darken slightly. "Mitch's attorney also sent over a new proposed custody agreement. Mitch is giving me full legal and physical custody of Linnie, and he doesn't want any holidays or summer vacations. He only wants to be able to see her if he occasionally travels to Raleigh on business."

I grimace over how cold this man is when it comes to his daughter. "I'm sorry. Have you talked to Linnie about that?"

Darby shakes her head. "Not until it gets finalized, but honestly, she's going to be okay with it."

"Maybe one day he'll wake up and realize how special she is," I offer to her.

"Maybe," she muses.

I draw Darby into me and wrap her in a hug. She returns it, and we stand that way for a long time. I think about my future and the place this woman will have in it. I think about Linnie, knowing she has a place right beside both of us. I vow silently to myself Linnie will always be a top priority with me. I won't be able to exactly make up for what she's missing from her father, but I sure as hell can give her love and security.

"I'd like to amend my previous statement," I murmur to Darby.

"What's that?" she asks, tightening her arms around me.

"The fall has been completed. I love you."

She hums low in her throat, or maybe it's a purr. Whatever it is, it doesn't matter. Because she gives me those words right back without any hesitation.

"I love you, too."

CHAPTER 29

Darby

Six weeks later

I RUN UP the porch steps and burst through the front door of Millie's. Three pairs of eyes all turn toward me. Larkin, who is on top of an eight-foot ladder stringing lit garland over the entryway into the sitting room; Morri D, who is standing at the bottom of the ladder and feeding more garland up to Larkin; and Laken, who is slouched sideways on one of the chairs filing her nails.

"Where's Mely?" I ask as I look around.

"She and Lowe left this morning," Morri says.

I do a double take at his outfit. He's wearing a winter white suit with a red lamè shirt underneath of it and a dashing piece of red lamé in the front pocket poking out. This is set off by the glittering red loafers and a white Fedora with a red lamé strip around it.

I nod at Morri's clothes. "You look festive."

"'Tis the season," he says with a snap of his fingers by his head.

Indeed.

'Tis the season.

We are five days away from Christmas, and Santa just came early today.

I had forgotten Mely and Lowe were taking a much over-due and needed honeymoon. They're going to St. Lucia for a week, and I envy them. Not because it's overly cold here in North Carolina, although there are some nights it can get down into the twenties, but because I have been working my butt off at the farm and I need a vacation myself. But that I can deal with later. This is much more important.

"So what's your news?" Laken asks.

Mely and Lowe opened Millie's Bed and Breakfast four weeks ago. They did an amazing job with the decorating and furnishing. When people walk in the front doors, they enter into a large foyer which was turned into a registration area. There's a curved writing desk with an elegant white leather chair that sits behind it. It holds a leather-bound registration book that guests fill in by hand. The old-fashioned and oversized brass keys to the four rooms upstairs hang on the wall. To the right is a large entryway that leads into a formal sitting room filled with plush seating. Heading through that room toward the rear of the house is another room Mely turned into a dining area. It has six round tables that each sit four people. To the left of the foyer is the kitchen, which is closed off to guests and has become Larkin's domain.

About two weeks after opening, Mely had approached Larkin about coming on as a partner in the business. The deal was she would not have to put any money in but would supply both time helping to run the place and coordinating the kitchen staff.

It turns out Larkin ended up doing a lot of the cooking and baking herself. Of course, she had to hire some extra help over at Sweet Cakes, but she said the money she made at Millie's more than offset it. Plus, she said she liked the challenge.

To everyone's surprise, Millie's ended up becoming a huge hit. While it wasn't completely booked every single night, at least three out of the four rooms were usually taken at any time. One of the things that drew people in was that Larkin started having a high tea every Thursday afternoon. This often brought in out-of-town visitors who wanted to get away for a few days and would stay throughout the weekend.

Morri walks up to me and snaps his fingers in front of my face, causing me to blink and focus in on him. "Morri to Darby... Morri to Darby... Come in, Darby."

I laugh and swat him away from me.

"It's final," I say with an excited shake to my voice, holding up the manila envelope that had just come in to the post office. I give a little squeal of excitement.

Larkin scrambles down the ladder and rushes toward me. She snatches the envelope out of my hands and digs into the opening I had torn into not long ago. She pulls out a multipage document stapled in the upper left corner. Holding it out, she reads it like a proud mom, "Final Divorce Decree."

"You're a free woman," Laken exclaims as she bounces off the chair and joins us.

Morri peers over Larkin's shoulder to look at the most beautiful document in the world. Mitch and I are now officially and legally over. Of course, he'll always be in my life to some extent. He does have to pay child support for Linnie, and I suppose there will be occasions where he wants to see her. So far since the entire spectacle went down with him torching Colt's farm, he has not asked to see Linnie once.

On the flip side, Linnie hasn't asked to see her dad either.

I find that incredibly sad because even though I'm not Mitch's biggest fan, I'm afraid he's going to end up having massive regrets one day. As for Linnie, she seems to be handling this better than I am. I've been told kids are more resilient than adults, and she is making me a believer.

These days, her life is filled with so much friendship and activity I have to keep a daily planner just so I know where my daughter is.

"Have you told Colt?" Larkin asks.

"He was the first call I made," I tell her. "We're going to eat dinner tonight at Clementine's to celebrate."

"So much for being a free woman," Laken mutters.

Larkin gives a slight punch to her sister's shoulder. "Be quiet. You have no reason to be teasing anyone when you act like a lovestruck fool every time Jake is around."

Laken blushes, and Morri laughs. Larkin holds up a finger as if she has a brilliant idea and says, "Champagne. This calls for champagne."

She dashes off into the kitchen, which is closed off from the foyer with a wooden swinging door.

While we wait for her, I point to the garland and ask, "Y'all are a little late in decorating for Christmas, aren't you?"

"Mely put up a Christmas tree in the formal room, but Larkin didn't think it was enough," Morri says with a huff. His tone is prissy and irate at the same time. "Why I'm down here volunteering my time and energy to decorate this place is beyond me."

"It's because you have a crush on the FedEx driver, Kelvin. Every time you come to visit, you order stuff to be delivered just so you can see him."

Morri gasps and flutters his hand over his heart. "That's a bald-faced lie."

Laken opens her mouth to retort, but all three of us turn in surprise when the front door to Millie's opens and a tall, muscular man fills the area. My eyes adjust to the glare from the sunlight behind him, and I immediately recognize him as the biker who had talked to Larkin and me several weeks ago.

He's dressed much the same way he was then, except he's got a little bit more gear on for the colder weather. He's wearing the black leather chaps, but the motorcycle jacket is thicker and comes down below his hips. There's a bandanna tied around his face just over his nose, presumably to keep the chilly air out as he rides, and he's actually wearing a black knit ski cap on his head.

Pulling his sunglasses off and the bandanna down so it hangs around his neck, his gaze focuses in on me for a moment before sweeping the interior foyer.

"Um… hello," I say after I unglue my tongue off the top of my mouth.

The man's gaze comes back to me, and he nods. "Got a room available?"

I glance at Morri, who is staring with his mouth hanging wide open at the huge biker. He doesn't necessarily look scared, but he does look wary. When I look at Laken, she is boldly running her gaze up and down him. I nudge her, and she mutters, "There's no crime in looking."

The kitchen swing-through door bursts open, and Larkin comes running through holding a bottle of champagne in her hand. She has the foil and wire cage removed, and she's in the process of trying to pull the cork. "I can't find any glasses. Let's just redneck it and drink from the bottle."

Larkin sees the biker and comes to an abrupt halt. The bottle of champagne falls out of her hands and hits the thick Chinese silk rug, which thankfully cushions it enough from breaking. However, the force of the impact causes the cork to shoot out, whereby it slams into the biker's calf. It looks like that could have really hurt had he not been wearing thick leather. As it is, he just looks down curiously at the cork lying on the floor.

Larkin doesn't move. She just stares wide-eyed at the biker while champagne continues to pour out all over the silk rug.

I scramble to pick the bottle up, completely amused over Larkin's reaction. When I stand, the biker is staring right back at her. I can tell by his expression he was hoping to see her.

Very interesting. In fact, I'd bet he came back to town *just* to see her.

"Um… Larkin…this gentleman would like a room. Do you have one?"

That seems to startle Larkin out of her daze, and she rushes behind the writing desk to open the leather-bound book in the center. "Um… of course we have a room."

The biker crosses the foyer to stand in front of the desk. Morri and Laken take three steps back to give him room. Larkin proceeds to flip to a blank page before taking a pen out of the desk drawer. She doesn't look up from the book, but starts asking the man questions.

"How long are you going to stay?"

"No clue," he says gruffly. "Until I get bored and decide to leave."

I find this to be fascinating, but Larkin stares at the blank pages of the registration book. "And would you like to add on a complimentary breakfast each morning?"

"If it's complimentary, why wouldn't I?" he asks.

Larkin still refuses to look at him. "Well, some people prefer to eat over at Central Café for a bigger type of breakfast. The complimentary breakfast is nothing but some fruit and pastries."

"I think I'll pass on the complimentary breakfast, then. If I want a pastry, I'll just walk over to that bakery I saw."

With her head still bowed over the book, Larkin continues this ridiculous conversation with him by saying, "Oh… that's my bakery."

"Really?" the biker says with clear amusement in his voice.

"That's right," Larkin says in a noticeably high-pitched tone. She still refuses to look at him and starts rambling on. "I opened it almost six years ago. I do mostly cakes and cookies, but I do some specialty items like seasonal pies."

To my surprise, the biker reaches a hand out and puts a finger gently under Larkin's chin, forcing her face up so she has to look at him. "You have pretty eyes. You shouldn't be hiding them."

"Oh, my word," Morri says dramatically. He turns to sashay into the sitting room while fanning his face with his hand. Taking a seat on the chair Laken had vacated, he watches the action with avid interest.

I eye Laken, and she smirks back at me.

Larkin seems to remember she was in the middle of registering a new guest, so she turns the registration book toward him. "If you would just fill this out."

The man bends over after pulling his gloves off and takes the pen from her. He scratches the information down and then pulls his wallet out of his back pocket. "I assume you need a credit card?"

Larkin nods as she turns the book back around to read what he wrote. She peers at it a moment, and then looks up to the stranger. "Deacon Locke?"

He grins at her. "That's my given name. But most people just call me Locke."

The front door to Millie's opens again, and we all turn to see Colt walking in. His eyes zero in on me, and he makes a beeline my way. "Saw your car out front. Thought I would come steal a kiss."

With no shame or embarrassment, Colt draws me into his arms, puts a hand to the back of my head, and lays a kiss on me that causes my toes to curl so tight I doubt I'll be able to walk again.

"That was nice," I murmur as he pulls away.

Colt smiles, but then looks over my head at the man we have just learned is called Deacon Locke. He nods at the guy and says, "What's up?"

Locke nods at Colt before turning back to Larkin. He hands his credit card to her. She takes it and runs it through a machine before handing it back to him. She then grabs one of the keys hanging behind her.

"Room number three. Top of the stairs, turn left, second door on the right. It has its own bathroom."

Locke nods and says, "I'll check it out later. Going to grab something to eat."

And with that, he walks out the door. There's nothing but silence for several long moments.

"Who the hell was that?" Colt finally demands of Larkin.

"Just someone who needed a room," Larkin mutters. She leans to the side to look out one of the glass panes beside the door. If I had to guess, her eyes are probably pinned to Locke's butt as he walks away.

I turn back to Colt, and he does not look happy about what he's witnessed so far. He's only seen a few seconds of the interchange between Larkin and Locke, but it's enough he's aware there is some serious chemical attraction going on between the two of them. Although if I had to guess, I would say Larkin probably doesn't quite understand Locke's view on things. She's not the most confident woman.

I can see Colt wants to grill his sister, and I decide I'm not going to let that happen. Grabbing his hand, I pull him into the kitchen.

"Are we still on for Clementine's tonight?"

"Is Linnie staying all night at the Goddard's?"

I give a coy smile as I nod, inching closer to him. His arms come around my waist, and his eyes twinkle with mischief. "Think you would be willing to have a sleepover at my place?"

I nod again. "Oh, yeah."

In the past six weeks, Colt and I have taken our relationship to a physical level. It was slow going, particularly given the fact I have a young daughter and our time together in a truly alone capacity is limited.

But once we got there… Oh, man. It was well worth the wait.

Colt tilts his head and brings his mouth to my neck. The kiss he gives me causes my entire body to shudder. He murmurs in my ear. "Then it's a date."

Pulling away from me, he says, "I've got some errands to run. Seven o'clock tonight?"

I nod effusively, wishing the hands of time would hurry up and move. "Can't wait."

Colt winks at me before he steps through the swinging door. "Do you love me today?"

He asks me that question every day, not because he has any doubts, but because it's just sort of become our thing.

"Every day and twice on Tuesday," I reply, which is how I always answer him.

"Love you too, babe," he says with a grin, and then he's gone from sight.

If you enjoyed *Pretty as a Peach* as much as I enjoyed writing it, it would mean a lot for you to give me a review on your favorite retailer's website.

Connect with Juliette online:
Website: juliettepoe.com
Twitter: twitter.com/juliette_poe
Facebook: facebook.com/AuthorJuliettePoe

About the Author

Juliette Poe is the sweet and swoony alter ego of New York Times Best Selling author, Sawyer Bennett.

A fun-loving southern girl, Juliette knows the allure of sweet tea, small towns, and long summer nights, that some of the best dates end sitting on the front porch swing, and that family is top priority. She brings love in the south to life in her debut series, Sex & Sweet Tea.

When Juliette isn't delivering the sweetest kind of romance, she's teaching her southern belle daughter the fine art of fishing, the importance of wearing Chucks, and the endless possibilities of a vivid imagination.

Made in the USA
San Bernardino, CA
15 March 2018